MAGIC EDGE

MAGIC EDGE

Dragon Born Alexandria: Book 1

www.ellasummers.com/magic-edge

ISBN 978-1-5175-3442-4

Cover art by Rebecca Frank

MAGIC EDGE

Dragon Born Alexandria: Book 1

Ella Summers

Books by Ella Summers

Dragon Born Serafina
1   Mercenary Magic

Dragon Born Alexandria
1   Magic Edge

Sorcery and Science
1   Enchanted
2   Wilderness
2.5   Menace
3   Machination
3.5   Revelations
4   Skybuilders

And more coming soon…

Read more at
www.ellasummers.com

Contents

CHAPTER ONE
Supernatural Showdown / 1

CHAPTER TWO
Paranormal Vigilante / 9

CHAPTER THREE
The Orbs of Essence / 15

CHAPTER FOUR
Impulse / 21

CHAPTER FIVE
Graffiti Dungeon / 30

CHAPTER SIX
The Assassin / 39

CHAPTER SEVEN
House of Thieves / 46

CHAPTER EIGHT
Magic Breaker / 56

CHAPTER NINE
House of Chocolate / 61

CHAPTER TEN
Supernatural Steel / 74

CHAPTER ELEVEN
Vampire Gunner / 81

CHAPTER TWELVE
Field of Fire / 86

CHAPTER THIRTEEN
Pixie Magic / 90

CHAPTER FOURTEEN
Assassin's Place / 101

CHAPTER FIFTEEN
Reckless / 109

CHAPTER SIXTEEN
Turned / 116

CHAPTER SEVENTEEN
Crimson Nightmare / 130

CHAPTER EIGHTEEN
The Convictionites / 141

CHAPTER NINETEEN
Iron Cage / 155

CHAPTER TWENTY
Blood and Chocolate / 163

CHAPTER TWENTY-ONE
The Dragon Summoner / 175

CHAPTER TWENTY-TWO
Secrets and Lies / 182

CHAPTER TWENTY-THREE
Swimming with Monsters / 188

CHAPTER TWENTY-FOUR
Magic Edge / 199

CHAPTER TWENTY-FIVE
The Aftermath / 210

CHAPTER TWENTY-SIX
Hidden Threat / 218

CHAPTER ONE

Supernatural Showdown

THE ONLY THING worse than a vampire was a vampire elf. And the only thing worse than a vampire elf was a whole gang of vampire elves, every last one of them worked up into a rage. They had the magic of elves and the bloodthirsty temperament of vampires. In other words, the species was a marriage made in hell.

But this wasn't Alex's first trip through hell.

She stood at the center of the open hall of Zurich's main train station. Hundreds of hushed voices echoed off the high ceiling, blending with the screech of braking trains and the hum of turning engines. The hall smelled of freshly baked pretzels and cigarette smoke—but most of all, it smelled of magic. The scents of mages and fairies were subtle but persistent, like the background buzz of a nearby highway. They were almost drowned out by the vampire elves' potent perfume of flowers and blood.

Just out of grappling range, they stood in a neat line, their red eyes pulsing with fury. They were clearly still grumpy about the rocks Alex had slingshot at them. As if to confirm this, the one with the thick nose ring lifted a hand

and gave the back of his head a tender pat. His fingers came back dripping blood.

"Stupid human woman," he growled, his voice crunching like shifting gravel. "You will pay for that." He slid the tip of his index finger into his mouth and licked it clean. Yuck.

Alex generally preferred her sword to a slingshot, but the vampire elves had run off as soon as she'd cornered them outside the jewelry shop they were looting. She trained everyday, but she wasn't as fast as a vampire or an elf. It took only a two-minute wheezy sprint for her to admit that to herself. So she'd switched to shooting pointy rocks at them.

It was hard to ignore a hailstorm of rocks, no matter how powerful you were. They'd stopped. And so here Alex was, locked in a supernatural showdown against a band of hybrid miscreants, smack dab in the middle of one of Europe's busiest train stations. Right at the peak of the five o'clock rush too.

A few curious passengers—tourists from the look of misplaced awe in their eyes—had paused along the sidelines to snap photos with their phones. One of them, a little girl with a black and pink Vampire Princess backpack, was capturing video with the grace and enthusiasm of a seasoned film auteur.

Most of the other passing people were either too rushed or too scared to join in. Zurich had always been a magical hotspot, but over the past few years, supernaturals had flocked there in record numbers. Mages, vampires, and fairies had practically taken over the city. For the most part, they were well-behaved; the Magic Council that ruled over the entire supernatural community didn't tolerate disorderly conduct. That's kind of what made them a dictatorship…or an oligarchy. Or whatever.

Anyway, despite all of this, there were still a few rebels. Alex was staring down a group of them now.

"If you turn and run off, we promise to give you a head start," Bloodfinger told her with a demented smile. "Maybe even five seconds."

"You've gone soft," said his lefthand neighbor, a woman with ears as pointy as her fangs.

"I'm just trying to make it interesting."

"That's the famed Paranormal Vigilante," Pointy said with a sneer. "A big, bad girl like her doesn't need five seconds."

Paranormal Vigilante. That's what the human population of Zurich had taken to calling Alex. She supposed the name was as good as any other. She kind of liked it actually. Ever since her arrival two months ago, she'd taken down more than her fair share of misbehaving monsters.

"That's right." Alex grinned at Pointy. "I don't need five seconds. I can take you all down in three."

Ok, so that wasn't exactly true, but most supernaturals appreciated bravado—or could at least understand it. Betray even the slightest hint of fear, on the other hand, and they'd stampede you like a pack of demon-possessed ponies.

"Do demonstrate." Pointy's grin grew pointier as she waved the others forward.

One of them sprang at Alex. He was fast—but he was also as dumb as dirt. She pivoted behind the airborne idiot and kicked him hard in the back. His face slapped the smooth floor with an echoing crack. The second guy attacked. Alex ducked to evade a punch whistling toward her head, spinning her leg as she dropped.

This vampire elf wasn't as dumb as the other; he rolled smoothly out of his fall. As he hopped to his feet, Alex unleashed her chain whip. She yanked him onto his companion, who was trying to peel himself off the pavement. She drew two long daggers and stapled the men together.

"You're a raving lunatic," Pointy said, her smile wilting.

"Paranormal Vigilante here." She pointed at herself. "It's all part of the job."

Alex tapped her fingers against the hilt of her sword, then motioned the final vampire elf forward. Besides Pointy, he was the only one left standing. The man was dressed in baggy shorts, a t-shirt with a magic gang symbol, and a backwards hat over shaggy hair. He didn't look a day over seventeen. For all she knew, though, he could have been two hundred. Vampires and fairies were both kind of eternal.

"Now hand over the bag before I stop playing nice," said Alex.

Bloodfinger took that moment to cough out a pained moan. Alex pulled out another dagger, and jammed it through the two guys, just to be safe. Mr. Backwards Hat, the vampire elf holding the backpack, took one look at his stapled friends, then began to slide the strap down his arm.

"Stop." Pointy caught his arm. "Don't let go of that backpack. No, on second thought, give it to me. You'll probably drop it."

Alex frowned at her. She didn't know what they'd stolen from the jewelry shop, but she *did* know that it wasn't theirs.

"Walk away," Pointy told her, swinging the backpack over her shoulders. "This is none of your business."

Alex's business right now was to hunt down the city's

misbehaving supernaturals. That's why she'd flown all the way from San Francisco to Europe. And stealing something out of a building owned by the League of Fairies definitely qualified as misbehaving. If she didn't reclaim whatever the vampire elves had stolen, the fairies would grind their bones into a stew. That just wasn't good PR—for anyone. The supernatural justice system was draconian at best, the punishments too gruesome for the human population to stomach.

"Sure this is my business." Alex clicked her tongue. "You've been naughty."

Pointy glared at her for a second, completely still. Then she threw back her hands and shot a blast of Fairy Dust at Alex. Sparkling like a crushed ruby and diamond rainbow, the ribbon of Dust cracked through the air. Alex rolled away, narrowly missing a face full of sedatives. The Dust bounced off the huge clock disc overhead, and hit the enormous mechanical timetable dangling from the ceiling. It groaned out a precarious croak—but held. For now.

Pointy shot another round at her. And another. Alex broke into a run and looped around, staccato bursts of crimson-coated Dust humming at her heels. A blast clanged against a metal trashcan, causing it to vomit up all its garbage. Crunched yogurt containers and brown banana peels erupted out of the top in an explosion of volcanic proportions. Alex hopped over the stream of garbage flowing down the escalator, then rolled to dodge the next blast. It didn't come.

Her magic exhausted, Pointy had stopped shooting. As the vampire elf shook out her hands, trying to recharge, Alex slid her fingers down to the knife at her thigh. She lifted it—

Pain pierced her neck. Alex reached back, trying to swat

Backwards Hat off of her. His fangs drilled deeper, holding on like a dog clinging to his bone. Venom poured through her veins, burning her blood and numbing her hands. She smacked him harder, but he still refused to budge. Purple and yellow spots danced before Alex's eyes. The muscles in her legs convulsed.

Magic shot past her ear, buzzing with electrical energy. Backwards Hat's grip broke. Alex turned and watched him stumble back, tendrils of red-gold lightning crackling across his chest before sizzling out. He took one look at the mage behind her, then bolted out of there.

"Alex," said a disapproving voice in a crisp British accent.

She glanced over her shoulder. Her friend Marek stood there, the tips of his spiky black hair frosted with red-gold lightning. He wore a black leather jacket with metal-studded lapels and half a dozen zippers. His off-white jeans sported at least as many zippers—most of them decorative—and his black combat boots had enough spikes to make a porcupine envious. A dozen rings sat on fingers exposed by fingerless leather gloves as smooth as creamed butter. He dressed like a total punk, but he spoke like a lord.

"Where's the other one?" she asked, looking around for Pointy.

"She scampered off while her mate was feasting on your blood."

Alex lifted her hand to the wound. Marek sighed with melodramatic flair, planting a hand on his hip.

"You're mad. Utterly mad, Alex." As he spoke, he waved the other hand about, drawing fiery patterns in the air. Showoff. "Why must you always look for trouble?"

Marek was half-British, half-Japanese, and one hundred percent old magic. His family was one of the most powerful in the mage community.

"It's my job to seek out trouble," she said. "That's what Gaelyn's paying me to do. And don't even try to pretend that you don't do the same. You're working for Gaelyn too."

"No, darling. I don't work for him. I'm indentured to him until I work off that favor my dear mum owes him."

"How long will that take?"

He shrugged. "Mum figures it shouldn't take more than a decade or two."

"A decade? Or *two*? Just what did Gaelyn do for her?"

"I believe it had something to do with cleaning up an army of ogres. Or was that trolls?" His honey-hazel eyes drifted upward in thought. "I can never remember. It's not really important. There are worse ways to work off a favor than doing the bidding of the world's most famous immortal philanthropist."

True. Supernaturals were a pretty high-strung bunch as a whole, but Gaelyn was super mellow. Maybe it was a consequence of his age. Rumor had it he was over six thousand years old.

"You're playing with fire, Alex," Marek said. "I can summon dragons and wield the power of the elements." He snapped his fingers, and a flame flared up. "You rely on poking monsters with your sword."

"And?"

"And what if they rip it out of your hands and poke you back?" he asked. "You need some long distance attacks when battling things faster and stronger than you."

"I have a slingshot."

He snorted. To his credit, it was a very posh snort.

"What are you doing here, anyway?" she asked. "I thought you had a flight to catch."

"I did, but then I heard you got it into your head to be

foolish again. I had to save you from yourself. You're human, not a mage."

So he thought.

"And yet you believed you could take on a gang of vampire elves with only your sword? You need to fight magic with magic."

"Magic like that from a first tier mage summoner such as yourself?"

"Naturally." His smile was far more modest than he actually was. "It's a good thing I came here to save you from becoming a vampire's snack."

"I had it under control." She swayed sideways.

"Alex?"

She tried to speak, but the words came out all garbled. Sweat soaked her face, dripping down her neck, where it burned against the blood bubbling out of her wound. The yellow and purple splotchy light show returned with a vengeance, and then the world went dark.

CHAPTER TWO
Paranormal Vigilante

THE GENTLE SLURP of water over rocks whispered in the distance, and sunlight warmed Alex's cheek. She cracked an eye open. The world had stopped spinning—for the most part. Black blotches solidified into jagged spikes of hair. Marek stood over her, the relief on his face quickly hardening into annoyance.

"You are out of your bloody mind," he said, throwing up his hands. "You know that, right?"

The ground shifted like a bowl of jelly beneath Alex as she tried to sit up. She forced her eyes the rest of the way open. She was lying on the waterbed in Gaelyn's guest room. The old immortal often waxed poetic on the revitalizing magic of water. That's why he had a house on the lake and kept a waterbed in his guest room. Sooner or later, anyone working for him got hurt.

"Did you carry me all the way here?" she asked Marek.

"I carried you to the train. You're heavier than you look."

Alex sat up. "It's all muscle."

"Yes, Wonder Woman. I know. I once made the

mistake of training with you."

She winked at him. "What happened on the train?"

"I put you into the seat next to me. A few of the passengers asked what had happened to you. I told them you'd passed out on account of your being pissed."

Drunk before sundown? Nice. "Thanks."

"Unfortunately, one of the passengers recognized you as the 'Paranormal Vigilante'." He gave his eyes a long, slow roll. "She was pretty excited. She even wanted your autograph. Her squeals attracted others. They wanted your autograph too. A few of them poked you for luck."

So that's why she'd dreamed of being squeezed like a bag of rolls at the supermarket.

"I reminded them that you were unconscious. They persisted. Then I told them if they didn't sod off and leave you in peace, I'd set the lot of them on fire."

"And did you?"

"I didn't have to. They turned out to be smarter than they looked."

"You're too hard on people," she said.

"When humans stop running into the middle of mage duels to capture video clips for their Youtube streams—or collecting debris from the battlefield for their junk collections—then I'll stop being hard on them."

"They didn't run into the middle of my fight with the vampire elves," she pointed out.

"A miracle of epic proportions." He set his hand on her forehead. "You're running a fever."

"It's the vampire venom," said Gaelyn, rolling a cart up to the bed.

Dressed in a set of beige robes and a matching hat that covered his long white hair, the world's oldest immortal was rocking the 'helpful and kind old wizard' look; maybe he'd been the one to invent the look in the first place some six thousand years ago. The tip of his waist-long beard tickled the top of his belt, from which hung a jagged dagger that looked more decorative than practical. Alex wouldn't have wanted to try to saw the head off a vampire with that garish thing.

"You've been poisoned, Alexandria. That's why you passed out," he said, handing her a cup of orange juice. "Drink this. You lost a lot of blood."

Alex lifted her hand to her neck. Her fingers rubbed over dried blood, but the wound was gone. She looked at him in surprise.

"Yes, your wounds have mended themselves. There was no need to heal you with magic."

Marek leaned in for a closer look, hissing as he saw her neck. "She's turning into a vampire?" He drew back, stretching out his hands to warm them up. Pink lightning sparkled on his fingertips.

"No," said Gaelyn. "I don't think so." His gaze shifted to Alex. "From what I can tell, your body appears to be fighting the vampire infection. It's eating it up, not the other way around. Remarkable."

"I've never heard of anything like that," Marek said, the tenor of his magic shifting with his mood.

Magic was a funny thing. For someone like Alex—someone who could sense magic—it could be seen and smelled and heard. It could be felt and even tasted. Every type of supernatural shared a common magical song. Vampire magic, for instance, popped and pounded like a heavy pulse. It was hot *and* cold. It slid and stroked like a river of crimson silk. There was something seductive about it, while at the same time repulsive.

At least this was true of the shapeshifting vampires and

the demon-powered vampires. Each of those two breeds had magic that resonated a little differently than the other. On the other hand, the third type of vampire—the so-called 'common' vampires—were hardly more than monsters, mere shells of their former selves. They served as the vampire elite's foot soldiers and reeked of rot and death. After any encounter with them, you had the sudden and immediate urge to shower.

"What exactly are you?" Marek asked her. "You claim you're human. But no human can take a bite like that and rise again. At least not rise again as one of the living." Suspicion flooded his magic.

Marek was a mage: a summoner and an elemental. His magic was firmly first tier, amongst the most powerful. He was currently ranked at #29 of all elementals worldwide and at #14 of all summoners. The #14 was because he could summon dragons—big, building-sized ones. There weren't a whole lot of mage summoners who could do that. It was considered the pinnacle of summoning magic.

First tier mages tended to come with egos to match their magic, but Marek wasn't all that bad most of the time. Like any member of a magical elite dynasty, though, he tended to be suspicious of things he couldn't explain. And Alex's body munching down on vampire venom wasn't something even she could explain.

"I've been bitten by a vampire before," she said.

"Really?" Waves rippled across the bed as Gaelyn sat down on the edge. He folded his hands together, his eyes intrigued. "When was this? What happened?"

"It was a couple of years ago. My sister Sera and I were working a job for Mayhem. A nest of common vampires had holed up in an old factory building. We went in to take them out. Sometime during the fight, one of them bit me.

He didn't hold on very long. I knocked him right off again. But it did sting."

"Did you run a fever? Pass out?" Gaelyn asked, his questions spilling out quickly.

"Yes to fever. No to passing out."

"Fascinating. Perhaps that small dose of venom allowed your body to work up some immunity to it. Like a vaccine."

Or maybe her Dragon Born blood, that which the Magic Council called an abomination, made her immune to vampire venom. There weren't many books that went into any great detail about the Dragon Born mages, and those that did were hidden away behind a million layers of 'restricted' signs at the library. The only way to read those books was to get a permission slip from the Magic Council. Yes, permission slip. Like they were all living in a freaking high school.

Alex wasn't going to ask for their permission. That would tip them off to what she was. And then they would execute her for the crime of being born.

"Yeah, vaccine," Alex said. "That could be it. Imagine if you could find a way to distribute a vaccine against vampire bites."

"Indeed. We could do those poor human victims a lot of good." Gaelyn's face was half mad scientist, half gleeful child. "I'll need to take some blood samples from you so I can research this further, Alexandria."

"Uh…"

"Yes, by all means, take *samples*," Marek ground out. "Why don't you invite the heads of all the nearby magic pharmaceutical companies to come over while you're at it? As though we don't already have a crisis on our hands!"

"Crisis?" she asked, grabbing onto that distraction for

dear life. Gaelyn was old, and if she was lucky, he'd forget all about his blood samples by the end of this conversation. Prominent immortal studying her weird blood equaled Magic Council SWAT team breaking down her door.

"Yes, crisis," said Marek. "Someone wants to annihilate every supernatural in the city."

CHAPTER THREE
The Orbs of Essence

ALEX THOUGHT IT seemed awfully nonchalant of her to grab a snack while the city was in peril, but a girl had to eat. That went double for girls getting ready to hunt down criminal masterminds. Based on her eight years' experience as a mercenary, she'd probably end the day splattered with blood and waist deep in monster goo.

"Ok," she said, sitting down at the bar opposite Gaelyn's kitchen.

They'd moved their little party into the enormous open living room. Light flooded through floor-to-ceiling windows on every wall, bathing her in warmth. It felt nice, like snuggling up to a soft, fuzzy blanket.

If the sun was still a friend to her, she probably wasn't turning into a vampire. Good. She was screwed up enough already without adding vampirism into the mix.

"Spit it out, guys," she said, biting the tip off her croissant. "Who wants to annihilate every supernatural in the city, and how will they do it?"

Marek exchanged glances with Gaelyn before he spoke. "I had a little chat with the pair of vampire elves you stapled together. After I made sure your wound had stopped gushing blood, of course."

She tipped her glass to him. "Appreciate it."

"You're lucky you're so odd, Alex. The bleeding stopped almost immediately. That wound was vile. It looked like a hell beast had torn a sizable piece out of your neck. Anyone else—even most mages—would have died from the blood loss. You just stopped bleeding." His dark brows drew together. "It was a good thing too. I'm a horrendous healer."

When Marek tried to heal someone, he ended up opening up new wounds as often as he managed to seal the existing ones. That's what happened when mages drew on magic outside of their core powers. Marek was one hundred percent a destructive mage. Even when he wanted to heal someone, his magic refused to go along with it.

About a week after she'd arrived in Zurich, they went to deal with a showdown between winged centaurs. Hybrid beasts had been popping up all over the city lately; that's one of the reasons Gaelyn had hired her. She had experience fighting freakish monsters.

During this fight of the winged centaurs, a woman had gotten caught in the crossfire, and Marek had tried to heal her. Her screams had only grown louder. Thankfully, they'd managed to get her to Gaelyn in time. But only barely.

"I mean this with all due affection, but don't ever try to heal me," she told Marek.

"I don't need to apparently. Not with your bizarre super healing."

Alex had magic. Legend said the Dragon Born had once been the most powerful mages in the world—well, before they were hunted to extinction. But she'd spent her whole life concealing her magic. She wasn't even convinced she was that powerful, no matter what those tall tales said. And she'd certainly never possessed super healing.

"So what did the vampire elves at the station tell you after you threatened to heal them?" she asked.

He stuck his tongue out at her. The tip of it was pierced. Ouch. That must have hurt.

"They said their gang stole the Fairy Orb from that jewelry shop," he said.

"Fairy Orb?"

"Think of it as a library of fairy magic," Marek said. "But instead of books, the Fairy Orb contains samples of every known fairy power."

Gaelyn handed her a weathered sheet of paper. Faded and wrinkled, it looked like it had spent a few weeks taped to a lamp post. "It's not just the Fairy Orb. A reward has been put out for the Orbs of Essence."

The paper sagged in her hand. She had to use both to hold it up. "The Fairy Orb, the Blood Orb, the Sorcery Orb, and the Otherwordly Orb," she read the names.

"The other three are the equivalents of the Fairy Orb for vampires, mages, and the otherworldly," Gaelyn told her. "Combined, these four orbs make up the Orbs of Essence."

"And what can you do with the Orbs of Essence?" she asked. *Please don't say 'summon the apocalypse'. Please.*

"Summon the apocalypse," Marek said.

Fantastic.

Gaelyn gave him a stern look. "Let's not exaggerate. Yes, long ago the Orbs could be used to hurt anyone with magic. That was millennia ago, though, and magic fades with time. Plus, it all depends how much the person wielding the Orbs knows about magic."

"And if they know a lot about magic?" Alex asked.

"Then they could wipe out the entire supernatural population of Zurich. Or one segment of the supernatural population. All the mages, for instance," said Marek. "The Orbs could be used to do the same to other cities. Bigger cities."

"In theory," Gaelyn amended. "And only worst case."

That 'worst case' sounded pretty damn grim.

"How can you stand there and act so calm?" Marek demanded, pacing.

"I got all the angst out of my system millennia ago," he replied.

Marek muttered something incomprehensible—but likely rude—under his breath.

"So who's after the Orbs?" Alex asked quickly, before he could say something he'd regret.

Usually, he and Gaelyn got along just fine, but Marek's heart was clearly back in London with his family. And when his heart revved up, his brain shut off and his mouth started running.

He must have been worried that once the perpetrators of this treasure hunt were finished with Zurich, they'd turn their eyes on other nearby cities. London would make a tempting next target. Its supernatural population was even larger than Zurich's.

"Maybe some supernatural group is trying to wage war on the others?" she added when no one said anything.

Marek gave up on his staring contest with Gaelyn. The old immortal looked more amused than annoyed, but that could change at any time. Even though he didn't have the temper of the younger supernaturals, there was only so much lip the grandfather of immortality could take from a hotheaded mage.

"I'd put good money on the vampires being the

culprits," Marek said. "They're a nasty lot with a long history of waging war on the other supernaturals."

"Alexandria will check it out," Gaelyn assured him, his gaze falling on the suitcase beside the front door. "You have a plane to catch. And you need to leave now, or you'll miss the last flight out today. Your mother has made it clear to me that she would not..." Gaelyn smacked his lips, searching for the right word. "...*appreciate* that happening again."

Marek snorted. "I'll bet. Did sweet old Maggie scare you?"

"Your mother is formidable."

"You have no idea." Marek walked to the door, his steps fluid but fast. "I'll be back in a few days, once the fun and games are over back home. Alex, try not to do anything reckless while I'm gone."

"I'm never reckless."

He turned toward her, hooking his hand around the handle of the suitcase. "Not even an hour ago, you got it into your head to shoot rocks at a gang of vampire elves."

She grinned at him. "It got their attention."

Marek looked at Gaelyn. "Try to talk some sense into her."

After he and his suitcase had rolled out of the house, Alex emptied the last of her orange juice. Someone had spread her knives across the dining room table—probably Marek from the looks of the mystical-looking pattern. She gathered them up.

"I'll look into the Orbs," Alex said as she sheathed the knives. "And try to figure out who put a price on them."

"That's a lot of knives," Gaelyn commented.

"Of course." She tucked the final knife into place. "I wouldn't want to be reckless."

"Where are you going?"

"To Impulse."

"That's a vampire bar," he said.

"Yes," she agreed. "Yes, it is."

CHAPTER FOUR
Impulse

IMPULSE WAS A vampire-owned bar in District 4. The clientele wasn't just vampires, though. The bar was the main watering hole for Zurich's supernatural population. On any given night, it was packed full of all sorts of them. Mages, fairies, vampires—this is where they came to mingle. When visiting the bar, it was best to look as menacing as possible. Leather and steel usually did the trick.

Especially when dealing with gruff bouncers.

"I don't know you," the muscle man grunted.

Alex looked down at the hand he'd clamped onto her, then peeled it off her arm. "You're new here," she said. "You weren't here when I came last weekend."

She was bluffing. Big time. She hadn't set foot inside Impulse in weeks, not since she and Marek had stopped by looking for a magic-drunk mage who got his kicks setting schoolhouses on fire.

"I started two days ago," he admitted, dropping his hand.

She nodded and gave him a big smile. It wasn't

surprising actually. The vampires at Impulse fell into two categories: those few long-timers who'd figured out how to pick their battles, and a revolving door of short-lasting newbies. Mr. Muscles here was of the latter category. He hadn't yet learned that immortality was no match for a room full of supernaturals drunk on magic cocktails. And self-entitlement, of course.

When Alex tried to pass him, he stepped into her path. "Supernaturals and their guests only, sweet pea."

She had her sword out and pressed to his neck before he could say 'vampire party mixer'. "I'm the Paranormal Vigilante." She shot him her best demented smile. "Perhaps you've heard of me."

"Yes," he said, low and quiet. He was trying really hard to keep his throat still beneath her blade.

"Let me pass."

As he shuffled aside, she lowered her weapon.

"Enter at your own risk, Paranormal Vigilante."

She glanced back at him. "What's that supposed to mean?"

"You're not the most popular person around here. Your reputation as a merciless cutthroat precedes you. The humans call you the Paranormal Vigilante. We supernaturals have a different name: Black Plague."

Alex snorted. "Cute. But the only people who have reason to fear me are those who've done something wrong. Does Impulse make a habit of harboring criminals?"

"No," he ground out. "Just watch your back in there."

"Is that a threat?"

"A disclaimer. Impulse takes no responsibility for your safety. Or death." A dash of crimson flashed briefly across his green eyes before fading out again.

"I'm a big girl. I can look out for myself."

A familiar flyer was tacked to the notice board behind Muscles—the Fairy, Blood, Sorcery, and Otherwordly Orbs bolded in thick, fancy letters. Alex pushed through the swinging door and entered the inner sanctum of Impulse.

Inside, spinning lights pulsed in time to the heavy bass beat. Bodies—only some of them alive—swayed and bounced on the dance floor. A trio of vampires sat in a lounge area off to the side, dipping bread cubes into a boiling pot of thick red fluid. Blood fondue. Yuck.

Alex plugged her nose before the stench of bubbling blood reached her, then headed for the bar. A group of fairies sat there, sipping sparkling pink and silver Fairy Dust cocktails while flirting with the bartender. Their dresses had only marginally more material than a Brazilian bikini, and they were using them to their fullest potential. His other customers forgotten, the bartender was practically drooling in the fairies' drinks.

A few stools down, a male mage in a russet cowboy jacket over a dark t-shirt was trying to get their attention by setting his drink aflame. And beside him, two summoner mages were making tiny dragons skip across the tabletop. The dragons' fiery forms reflected off the glass fronts of the liquor cabinets behind the bar. Ghosts floated overhead, their translucent bodies dancing in swirling, shimmering loops to the music.

A song with a chirpy, bubblegum beat came on. The fairies jumped up and stormed the dance floor, much to the bartender's dismay. Alex swooped in and took one of their seats.

"Hello, pretty," said the drunk cowboy mage, leaning sideways to wrap his arm around her shoulder. He smelled like elemental magic and freshly cut grass. Burning grass.

Alex shrugged him off. "Your drink is on fire, hotshot."

"You think that is hot?" He waved his hand over his drink, and the flames blazed higher. "I'll show you the meaning of hot."

Oh good, an idiot. She kept her face neutral. She'd not come here to break noses.

"I'll set your sheets on fire."

On the other hand, some people were just asking for it.

"…burn the clothes right off you…"

Since when was being roasted alive a turn on?

"…your blood will boil…"

This was just getting better and better.

"…your skin scorch—"

"Hold your horses there, cowboy," she cut in. "I don't know about you, but where I come from, girls don't enjoy being set on fire."

He leaned in, wetting his lips. "And where's that?"

"San Francisco."

"San Francisco?" His flame went out. "You're her. The Black Plague."

She flashed him a grin. "I prefer Paranormal Vigilante."

Without another word, the Cowboy stumbled off his stool and power-walked out of there. Either he'd been hit with the sudden urge to pee, or he was going to find a new hiding place for the packs of magical weeds stuffed inside his jacket's inner pockets. He needn't have bothered. Gaelyn only sent her after monsters and thieves, not drug dealers—not even drug dealers who dressed like cowboys.

"I've never seen Jack give up on a woman so easily," the bartender said as he stopped in front of her.

"His name is Jack?"

"Yes. Why? Planning on hunting him down?"

"No." She nearly gagged on her own tongue. "Jack the Cowboy? It's just all wrong. Jack the Pirate maybe."

His laugh was deep and pleasant—well, for a vampire, anyway. Just like the bouncer at the door, this guy's magic had the elasticity of a shifter. If not for the heavy pop of blood magic, he might have been almost charming.

"What can I get you?" he asked.

Alex was hit by the sudden craving for a magic smoothie—or maybe that was just homesickness. "Pineapple juice."

"So, what can you tell me about the Orbs of Essence?" she asked as he poured ice into a glass.

His hand froze over the glass. "Pardon?"

"The Orbs of Essence. Someone is after them."

"I don't know anything about that."

Liar. The beat of his magic sped up, giving him away.

"Are you absolutely sure you don't know anything?" she asked. "Because the reward notice is posted on the message board at the front."

"Is it?" His magic was galloping. He poured the juice over the ice. His hand shook, and he spilled a little. "Here you go."

Then he walked over to the mage summoners he'd been ignoring up until now. Yeah, he knew something. Alex was about to test that theory, when someone slid onto the barstool next to hers.

"Vigilante."

Alex knew that voice, and she wished she could have ignored him. But you didn't ignore assassins, especially not an assassin who'd taken it upon himself to make her life a living hell ever since her arrival in Zurich. She turned her head and gave him a curt nod.

"Slayer."

That's what people called him. If he had another name, she didn't know it. And she didn't want to.

"You certainly have a way with people," he said, his gaze darting briefly to the bartender before returning to her. His eyes were as green as the deep jungle—and just as deadly.

"Oh, assassins have great people skills?"

"I'll have you know that mine is a time-honored profession." His accent was frosted with a hint of something different. Australian? British? It wasn't strong enough for her to be sure.

"That doesn't answer my question."

"No." He chuckled. "I suppose it doesn't."

Alex took a sip of her juice. It was unusually sweet but still delicious. "What's put you in such a good mood? Kill someone today?"

"Not today." A cool smile slid up his lips. "Not yet anyway."

"I'm armed," she warned.

His eyes panned up her legs. "I can see that. Eight knives by my count, plus the sword. Planning on storming an enemy encampment tonight? Or do you just enjoy playing Warrior Princess?"

She sighed. "What do you want, Slayer?"

"Do I have to want something to pay my dear friend, the Paranormal Vigilante, a visit?"

"Yes. You never do anything without some sinister reason."

"You don't like me very much."

"No."

Swiveling his seat around to face her, he set his hand over his heart in mock despair.

"You're a brutal killer," she said.

"We're a lot alike, you and I."

"We're *nothing* alike. You kill for profit. Or pleasure. I

don't even know," she spat back, taking another sip before she could say something really nasty.

"Perhaps all the press has gone to your head, Vigilante. You are a mercenary. You fight for profit." He leaned in, whispering, "But you know what I think? I think you like it."

"I don't—"

"The thump of your heart." His breath caressed her skin, hot and thick. "The rush of adrenaline. Blood pumping to every part of your body." He traced a finger down her arm. "It's a high like no other."

"I—"

"Well, almost no other," he whispered against her cheek.

Then he pulled back, his smile smug, his eyes indecent. He was playing her. Again. Alex resisted the urge to kick him in the shin. She settled for kicking his chair. As it began to spin, he caught his hand on the bar, pushing himself back around to face her.

"Let me order you a drink," he said.

"So you can poison me? I don't think so."

"You wound me. If I wanted to poison you, I wouldn't have let you see me first."

"Sure you would have. Your ego demands seeing your victim die."

He expelled a heavy sigh. "I promise I won't try to kill you."

"Your word as an assassin?"

"Yes."

"Sorry, but I just don't trust you. Your promises last only as long as your next assignment. You have no problem selling out to the highest bidder."

"Nice boots," he said, looking at them. "Are they new?"

"What?"

"The first time I saw you, your shoes were peeling and your clothes were torn. Nowadays, you walk around in fancy boots and designer threads. Working for Gaelyn must pay well."

"What's your point?"

"That you're a mercenary. You yourself have no problem selling out to the highest bidder."

"Gaelyn is a philanthropist. He's hired me to hunt down monsters and supernaturals who hurt people. Your clients hire you to kill people they don't like. If someone offered you enough to take out the Paranormal Vigilante, you wouldn't even hesitate."

"I don't know about that. I might hesitate a little."

She glared at him. "You think this is funny, do you?"

"Of course it's funny. This whole thing is completely absurd. No one could pay me enough to go after you."

"Oh, like me that much?"

"Yes, there's that." He winked at her. "But mainly I just don't want to go toe-to-toe with you. You fight mean."

"Not as mean as you do."

"I don't know about that. I saw you staple those vampire elves together with your daggers."

She downed the rest of her drink. "You were spying on me?"

"Observing from the shadows."

"Like any good assassin?"

"Naturally."

She snorted.

"I appreciate the way you fight. I've rarely met anyone so skilled, Alex."

"How do you know my name?"

"I know a lot about you, Alexandria Dering."

She laughed so hard, she nearly fell out of her stool. He moved forward to catch her.

"What's so funny?" he asked.

"I don't really know," she laughed, burying her face against his chest. It was as hard as granite and smelled of warm spice and amber. She inhaled deeply and picked up a hint of leather and orange too. He smelled sexy enough to eat.

"Alex."

She looked up. "Yes?"

"Come with me."

"Hmm? Why?"

"You aren't yourself right now. It's dangerous for you to stay here when you're like this."

She snickered. "I'm fine."

When she tried to stand up, she stumbled to the side, barely catching herself on the bar. The room was a blotchy canvas of pulsing streaks. It hadn't been spinning so much when she'd come in, had it?

You've been drugged, a voice said in her head.

She laughed at it.

Snap out of it.

"Ok, then," she said. "I'll just be going now."

She blacked out. The next thing she knew, Slayer had her cradled in his arms, and he was carrying her toward the exit.

"Put me down," she said, her words slurred and sloppy. Her pulse pounded in her ears.

When he didn't say anything, she tried glaring at him— but her eyes weren't working. She couldn't see anything but the pitch black abyss.

"What have you done to me?" she growled right before she passed out.

CHAPTER FIVE
Graffiti Dungeon

ALEX OPENED HER eyes to find an angel with golden hair and a halo of emeralds staring at her. It wasn't a real angel, of course. He'd been painted onto the wall, along with fairies and vampires. In the background, a herd of unicorns battled it out against some dark ponies with teal-green bodies, purple manes, and golden hooves that dripped blood.

The room was cast in shadows, but there was just enough light to see that supernatural motifs covered every wall. The colorful graffiti contrasted starkly with the bare, ugly concrete of the floor and ceiling. Early morning light cut through the slender window slits.

She'd been here all night. Wherever 'here' was. She started for the door—only to be yanked back by the chains locked around her wrists and ankles. Metal rattled as she shook her hands, but the chains held. They were attached to the ceiling. The pair around her ankles were bolted to the floor. She wasn't even wearing shoes anymore. Her sword was gone too. So was her leather jacket with all her knives. And the knives she'd hidden elsewhere on her body.

"Damn assassin," she growled. He'd done a thorough job of disarming her. That made her almost as mad as being chained up in some creepy basement. Without her weapons, she might just as well have been naked.

"Let's not go calling names now," Slayer said, stepping out of the shadows.

There was something odd about his aura. He didn't feel supernatural, at least not like any supernatural being she'd ever met—but he didn't feel completely human either. There was magic in him.

"I know what you are," he said.

Alex's heart stuttered in her chest. Eight years ago, an assassin had killed her father. He'd been after her and Sera, but he didn't have any problem mowing down anyone who got in the way.

Dad had gotten in the way. That was the only time Alex had used her magic to kill. Looking down on her father's broken body, rage had taken over. The magic she'd spent years concealing flooded out of her. She'd blasted the assassin so hard that he was dead even before he hit the wall. The knowledge of her forbidden origin had died with him.

Or so she'd thought.

Was history repeating itself? Had Slayer found out that she was Dragon Born? Is that why he'd been stalking her for weeks, just waiting for the right moment to strike? Turning her in to the Magic Council was worth a bounty of at least two million dollars—and the leaders of the supernatural community weren't too choosy if she arrived on their doorstep dead or alive. They'd kill her themselves anyway.

"I know what you are," he repeated, drawing closer.

Alex didn't have an answer for that. "What the hell did you do to me?" she demanded, using anger to drown out her fear.

"I did nothing. It was Hugh."

"Hugh? Who's that? Is it the name of your alter-ego?"

"No." A chuckle rumbled deep in his chest. "That's the bartender at Impulse. He poisoned your drink."

She frowned. "I knew he was lying."

"Pardon?"

She shook her head. "Nothing. How did you know he was the one who poisoned me? Maybe it was a certain assassin."

"Me?" He laughed. "I don't poison people, doll. What's the challenge in that?"

Yep, he killed for pleasure too.

"I know it was Hugh because I asked him about it after you passed out," Slayer said. "He meant to kill you. Apparently, you were asking the wrong questions. But you survived the poison. How?"

Wouldn't I like to know. It was just like the incident with the vampire venom. Her body had fought that off too.

"What kind of poison did he use?" she asked him.

"The Black Death."

That poison came from the thorns of a magical rose plant. It was fast-acting, mostly tasteless, and one hundred percent deadly.

"Hugh probably saw poetic irony in using the Black Death to kill the Black Plague," Slayer said.

Alex scowled. She'd show that homicidal ass some poetic irony when she punched him in the face.

"And yet you survived. How?" he asked.

"Just lucky, I guess." The chains jingled as she shrugged back her shoulders.

"Hmm."

He flipped a knife up in the air, then caught it. A jolt of

anger ripped through her as she recognized her own weapon.

"That's mine," she growled.

"Yes. And what a very pretty knife it is," he replied. "But stop changing the subject."

"I don't know how I survived the poison, and even if I did, I wouldn't tell someone who sells secrets as well as takes lives."

"Touché."

"Why did your friend Hugh feel the need to poison me anyway? He could have just ignored me."

"He's not my friend. He's a source of information," Slayer said dispassionately. "After I dropped you off in my car, I went back to ask him about it. He said you were snooping for information about the Orbs of Essence."

"Snooping?"

"It turns out that while I was carrying you to my car, some guys came into the bar and stole the Blood Orb out of the vault."

"The Blood Orb was being stored at Impulse?" she asked, feeling stupid. She could sense magic better than most anyone. Why hadn't she sensed the Blood Orb?

Because you allowed yourself to get distracted flirting with the assassin, the voice in her head said.

She didn't try to argue with it. The damn thing was right. And she was an idiot.

"Yes, it was Impulse's turn to store the Blood Orb," he said. "They'd had it for only two nights before someone stole it. Rumor has it the Vampire Covenant is in a real temper right now."

So the vampires weren't behind the thefts like Marek had thought. Or it was rogue vampires after the Orbs.

"Hugh knew Impulse would be hit last night," Alex

realized. "That's why he was so jumpy when I started asking questions about the Orbs. He was afraid I'd figure out he was helping the thieves and that I'd turn him in."

"He claims he poisoned you because he thought you were one of the thieves after the Orbs of Essence."

"He's such a liar."

"Yes. When vampires lie, their scent changes. You can taste it in the air. It takes on a subtle hint of burning metal."

Alex had thought she was the only one who noticed that.

"He looked far too relieved when I told him I'd taken you out of there," he said.

"Did you tell him that I'd survived his poison?"

"No, he didn't need to know that." Slayer gave her a smile as deadly as he was. "I saved you from a most unpleasant fate."

"My hero," she said drily, rattling her chains for emphasis.

She'd broken chains before. It just took time—and a touch of magic. She eased her magic down the thick silver links, making it eat away at the steel.

"Come now. Don't be moody."

"Moody?" she spat back his words. "I was poisoned—"

"Which wasn't my fault."

"—and then I woke up in a dungeon tied down with chains. I have every right to be moody!"

"After you passed out, you developed a slight fever. It didn't seem serious, but your body put you to sleep to fight the poison. It didn't look like you'd regain consciousness before morning. If I hadn't restrained you, you would have tried to take my head off the moment you woke up. And knowing your temper, you wouldn't have even bothered to ask questions first. At least this way, we could have a civil conversation."

"I'm in chains, you deranged assassin! There's nothing civil about it."

"I've seen you fight, Alex. You're strong, agile, and smart. Normal restraints wouldn't hold you," he said calmly. "And, yes, this is the most civil conversation we've ever had, barring last night. You should throw yourself at me more often. It's endearing."

"I didn't throw myself at you. I fell off my stool because I'd been drugged."

"And I suppose you're going to blame the rest of your behavior on the drugs too?"

"The rest of my behavior?" The details of last night were foggy. She hoped she hadn't done anything...inappropriate.

"Inhaling my scent." He smile smugly. "Calling me sexy. There may have been some touching."

Alex wished her hands were free so she could cover her mortification by throwing a few daggers at the wall. But they weren't, so she had to settle for looking daggers at the assassin.

"I don't recall anything of the sort," she said.

"Then I'll just have to remember for the both of us." His smile grew wider, teetering on rapturous. "I'm glad we're finally having this talk. It's long overdue."

As overdue as a magical apocalypse—and just as welcome.

"You've been blowing me off for weeks," he said.

"I've suffered through more than my fair share of conversations with you, Slayer."

"Logan."

"That's your real name?"

"Yes."

She chuckled.

"You find my name amusing, do you?"

"It's not the name of an assassin."

"Hence my choice of Slayer," he said. "My parents didn't name me with the expectation that I'd one day become an assassin."

"How do you know? Did you ask them?" she teased.

"They told me so. Right before they disowned me."

"Oh."

She tried not to think about it. She was *not* going to feel sorry for an assassin. Especially not the assassin who'd locked her up in his dungeon. She tested the chains. The metal had softened, but not yet grown brittle.

"Well, Logan, I don't see any need for us to discuss anything. You tried to kill me the first time we met, and I don't see any evidence that your morals have changed since then."

"There's no need to hold a grudge, princess. That was a simple misunderstanding, nothing more."

"A misunderstanding," she stammered out. "Was it a *misunderstanding* that you snuck up on me and tried to jump me in a dark alleyway?"

He shrugged. "We were after the same target that day. Once we realized that, we ended up killing the monster together, remember?"

Of course she remembered. It was hard to forget. There weren't many people who could move like Logan. He fought like a demigod.

He moved in closer, his breath hot on her skin as he whispered into her ear. "You're attracted to me, Alex. Just admit it." As he pulled away, his cheek brushed against hers.

Repressing a shiver, she hardened her eyes and glared at

him. Chains clinked together as she crossed her arms to her chest. Almost there. She started to work her magic on the chains holding her feet. "Attracted to you? Puh-lease! I will admit no such thing."

"Stubborn woman."

"Demented assassin."

He grinned.

"What do you want?" she demanded. "Why am I still chained here?"

"What will you do if I release you?"

What indeed? She saw herself dislocating his shoulder. If he was really mean, she might even break it. Come to think of it, he deserved a broken rib or two as well. And maybe a punch to the kidney.

"What I'll do depends on what you want," she told him.

Still smiling, he took another step back. "You accuse me of being mad for enjoying a good fight. But I saw that gleam in your eyes just now. You were thinking of headbutting me."

Yeah, and he'd ruined it by moving out of range. "Let's just get to the point."

"You're investigating the Orbs of Essence," he said. "And doing a pretty piss-poor job of it too. I knew what you were after the moment you fumbled your attempt to interrogate the bartender. If almost everyone at Impulse last night hadn't been completely smashed, they'd have noticed it too."

"My speciality is fighting, not interrogating."

Logan snorted. "That much is obvious. You're about as subtle as a punch to the gut."

Alex glowered at him.

"You want to know what's going on with the Orbs of

Essence. Well, so do I," he said. "Due to the high bounty, there are dozens of hunters after the Orbs. That band of vampire elves were just the beginning. Together, we can stop those amateurs from getting their hands on them. What do you say?"

"You're an assassin," she pointed out.

"And a thief, don't forget," he said. "You're working with Gaelyn. That old man has deep pockets. He can afford my fee."

"I don't trust you."

"I can live with that."

"Maybe I can't live with that," she said. "I don't want to be constantly on the lookout, watching for the inevitable stab in the back."

"I won't betray you."

"No, you won't. Because I won't give you the chance to," she said, yanking on her chains. They broke off at her wrists and ankles, crumbs of shredded steel snowing down to the ground. "Now, hotshot, let's see what you've got."

CHAPTER SIX

The Assassin

TRUE TO HIS profession, the assassin moved like silk and hit like stone. Alex barely had time to evade the first fist he hammered at her head. She wasn't quick enough to evade the second; it pounded hard against her ribcage and sucked the breath right out of her lungs. She stumbled back in retreat, gasping for air.

"This isn't going quite like you'd pictured it, is it?" he said, the hint of a chuckle speckling his words. He didn't move in, even though he could have taken her out pretty easily right now.

"No," she growled. "It really isn't."

She angled a kick toward his shin. He sidestepped with a fluidity that took years to master—and few ever did. She tried for his head next. When he evaded that too, she switched to his shoulder. That didn't work either. Logan was too fast and too strong. And he was really starting to get on her nerves.

"What are you?" she asked. "A vampire hybrid? A shifter mage?" Neither of those sounded quite right.

"I'm not magical. I'm human," he replied.

She could hardly hear him over the pounding drum beat of her pulse.

"Albeit a genetically-enhanced human," he added.

"Enhanced?" she asked. "Enhanced for what?"

"Strength, endurance, speed—basically everything I'd need to take down a supernatural."

"I've never heard of such a thing," she said.

Not that she was surprised such people existed. Many humans didn't like the idea of being so vulnerable to the supernaturals. It was only a matter of time before someone managed to develop countermeasures.

"The world is full of surprises," he said.

Grinning, Alex aimed a kick at his groin. Even the badass assassin Slayer was a man underneath it all. He was too experienced to put up a hand for her to kick into him, but instinct compelled him to protect himself. As he hopped back, she swept her leg across the ground, kicking his feet out from under him the moment he landed.

He fell—but not far. He braced his hands against the floor and flipped back up to his feet. It just wasn't fair. No one was that good.

"There's no need to work against each other when we could work together," Logan said, circling around her.

She matched him step for step. There was no way she was letting someone that fast out of her sight. She'd probably wake up in chains again.

"We would make a good team," he continued. "My knowledge and experience combined with your magic."

Alex froze, remembering to move again just in time to narrowly miss a nasty punch to the face.

"I know you have magic," he said. "Don't even try to deny it. Only someone with magic could have done *that* to those chains." He pointed at the frayed ends of shredded metal dangling from her wrists and ankles like demonic jewelry.

"Maybe I used a chemical agent."

"No," Logan said. "I checked you. Thoroughly."

The look in his eyes was provocative, the smile on his lips outright wicked. Alex nearly blushed—until she remembered that she wasn't attracted to him. Not at all. At least not most of the time. Well, maybe only occasionally.

Ok, fine. If sex had a face, he would be it. His aura screamed power, raw and turbocharged. Maybe he wasn't made of magic, but there was definitely something magical about him. Especially those eyes. They burned with green fire. She wanted to throw him against the wall and just—

"Why do you hide your magic?" he asked, his words stomping that thought right out of her.

"There's nothing to hide," she replied. "Because I have no magic."

"You're not human."

"Neither are you," she said. "Maybe I'm a genetically-engineered super human, just like you."

"Cute, Alex. Nice try. But as you might imagine, I know a thing or two about genetically-engineered super humans, and you aren't one of us."

"There are more of you?"

"Yes."

"How many?"

He looked at her for a moment, as though he was going to say something, but then he shook his head. "No. Not yet."

"Why not?"

"You don't trust me, so I can't afford to trust you."

"Fine," she said. "Let's just get this fight over with."

"As you wish." His hand darted forward, obviously

aiming for her solar plexus.

Oh, no you don't! She'd had the wind knocked out of her enough times today already. The broken remnants of her ankle chains swooshed against her legs as she spun out of the way. Logan's momentum drew him forward, past her. Now in back of him, she swung out the chains dangling from her wrists. They hooked around his arms, and she heaved back. She looped her arm around his head, holding him in a solid lock.

"Got you," Alex said in triumph. He wouldn't be breaking out of that hold, no matter how strong he was.

"So you do. Congratulations. It almost makes you forget about that major blow to the ribcage I landed on you, doesn't it?"

She scowled at him, only to realize that he couldn't see her expression with his back to her. Phooey. "I beat you fair and square."

"Using weapons."

"Weapons? What weapons?" she asked.

"Those chains."

"You mean the chains you used to tie me up in your basement?"

He expelled a patient sigh. "Well, when you say it like that, of course it sounds bad."

"It doesn't just sound bad. It *is* bad," she told him. "A normal person doesn't chain people up in his basement. That's the realm of serial killers and other psychopaths."

"I'm a genetically-engineered assassin designed to kill supernaturals. I have super strength and speed, and I've trained to fight my entire life. When did I ever claim to be normal?"

"Well...you didn't. I suppose."

"And as I explained to you, I saved you from death last

night. The least you could do is say thank you."

"Thank you," she muttered.

"You're welcome. Now let me go, so we can talk like civilized people."

Alex loosened her hold but didn't let go entirely.

"Or would you rather keep fighting it out like barbarians?" he asked.

"Fine," she said, releasing him.

He pivoted around to face her. "Damn it, Alex. That hurt." He rolled his head around slowly, stretching it out.

"Good. Maybe now you'll think twice about chaining people up."

He sighed. "Let me see your hands."

She showed them to him. A red rash ring was burned around each of her wrists. Logan unlocked the clamps, and they fell to the ground. He brushed his finger across her wounds.

"That bad?" he asked.

"No," she lied through clenched teeth. She tried to relax her face—to hide the pain—but her skin was as raw as an uncooked steak.

"I have a cream that might help with that," he said.

"No, thank you. I've been poisoned quite enough times for one week."

"Are you trying to be difficult, or are you just naturally that way?"

"That depends. Are you trying to be obtuse, or are you just naturally that way?"

"That smart mouth is going to get you into trouble someday," he told her.

"Thanks for the warning, but it's about twenty years too late. That day has long since come and gone. But if you stick around long enough, it will surely come again." She shrugged. "It happens at least once a week."

His blond eyebrows lifted. "You'd like me to stick around?" He looked happy, but you never could tell with assassins.

Err... "I said a week, Romeo, not a lifetime."

"Romeo, huh?"

She tapped her fingers across her arms and waited for him to get to the point.

"I don't like Romeo," Logan said. "He mopes about, spouting silly poetry. Then he kills himself with poison because he's an idiot."

"There are a few things in between."

"Yeah, more poetry." He rolled his eyes. "And more killing."

"Assassins are no strangers to killing."

"No, we're not," he agreed. "But we are strangers to getting ourselves killed due to idiocy. At least the good assassins are. The others are dead, so I can't ask their opinion of poetry. Or poison."

She tried hard not to laugh—but only half succeeded. A garbled chortle burst forth from her lips, and she turned it into a cough. Logan didn't look fooled.

"I take it from the fact that you haven't resumed your efforts to chain me to you, that you've agreed to take my help in finding the Orbs," he said.

"Why do I need your help? What can you contribute? Besides the assassin jokes, that is."

"You want to work with me because I have contacts. I'm in the same circles as the people who will be after that bounty on the Orbs."

"Circles of assassins and thieves," she said. "Forgive me if I don't find your association with them particularly comforting."

"Don't worry, I'll protect you."

This time, she didn't even try to hide the laugh. In fact, she added an extra sarcastic kick to it.

"Look, all that matters is I can get you close to people who might know something about who's after the Orbs," he said. "You can take my offer. Or not. But if you don't, I might decide to collect on that bounty myself."

Alex sighed. "Fine. You might be useful after all, but I'll need to run it by Gaelyn first. Where's my stuff? I'm going to forewarn you now. If you tell me you've already pawned it off, I promise I'll retaliate in kind."

"Relax. It's in the other room. Just what sort of assassin do you think I am?"

CHAPTER SEVEN
House of Thieves

AS IT TURNED out, Logan was the sort of assassin who had your stuff cleaned and neatly sorted—you know, after he chained you up in his basement. Alex strapped on all her blades, just in case the assassin decided he'd like to kill her after all. Assassins were fickle like that. She took a moment to greet her boots and then dialed Gaelyn's number.

"Alexandria," the immortal answered in his calm, grandfatherly voice.

"Hi. So I kind of got tied up last night." In an assassin's basement. "That son of a harpy who bartends at Impulse poisoned me."

"Alexandria, you must be more careful. That's twice in one day. You're putting undue stress on your body."

Yeah, like she'd asked the vampire elf to bite her, then had run over to Impulse and told the bartender to put poison in her pineapple juice. Gaelyn didn't coddle his employees. He was a no-nonsense sort of grandfather. Alex had never met either of her grandfathers, but she imagined they must have been just like that.

"I feel ok," she said, opening and closing her fists. She

46

hopped a few times on one foot, then switched to the other. "All systems in order."

"I'd still like to take some blood samples to be sure. Your reaction to the vampire venom was most unusual."

So he hadn't forgotten about that after all. Damn. "Blood samples. Right. When I have time." Which would be never, if she could help it. "But I'm not calling about the poison."

"I've heard about the theft of the Blood Orb from Impulse last night."

His tone was perfectly neutral, but Alex couldn't help but feel defensive. Probably because she felt guilty.

"Yeah, that happened while I was out from the poison," she said. "You might want to tell the vampires about the bartender who betrayed them."

There was a brief pause. "Done."

Through magical or technological means? Alex didn't ask. Gaelyn was pretty handy with a smartphone—for an old guy.

"Wait, a minute," Gaelyn said. "The vampires say the bartender is already dead. Someone found his head in the back room of the bar this morning."

Yuck. "And the body?"

"Not yet."

It sounded like someone was tying off loose ends.

"Anything else, Alexandria?" Gaelyn asked.

Logan entered the room and leaned against the wall.

"Uh, yes." She chewed on her lip. "I've found myself a...partner."

The assassin winked at her.

She stuck her tongue out at him. "Someone to work with me in the investigation."

"Who?"

"Slayer."

"The assassin?" Low chuckles rumbled from the other end of the line. "I thought you two hated each other."

"Yeah, well, I guess we'll have to look past that to achieve our common goal," Alex said, looking at Logan.

He rubbed his fingers together.

"Right, so there's just one little thing."

"The assassin wants to be paid," Gaelyn said.

"He claims to have contacts in the criminal underworld who might know who's after the Orbs."

"Of that I have no doubt."

"So, what should I tell him?"

For a moment, Gaelyn didn't say anything. As the grandfather of the supernatural community, he always worked to keep them safe. Oftentimes, that meant sending Alex or Marek or someone else after monsters or misbehaving supernatural citizens. He wasn't part of the Magic Council. He was outside of it—above it in many ways because he was so much older than anyone else. The Council members respected him. When he said something, they listened. And he'd told them to keep the supernaturals in check and the humans safe. That was the only way to keep the peace.

Alex wasn't sure what exactly Gaelyn was. He wasn't a mage or vampire or fairy. And he wasn't one of the otherworldly. She did know that while Gaelyn was immortal, his magic had dwindled with the passing years. He didn't talk about it much, but Marek had told her.

What Gaelyn lacked in magic, though, he more than made up for in money. He'd accumulated a lot of wealth over the millennia and had no problem spending it to protect the supernatural community, even from itself. But he didn't have much love for assassins.

"All right," he finally agreed. "Tell your assassin that I'll pay him for his assistance. But do be careful, Alexandria. Assassins are dangerous enemies and even more dangerous friends. Watch your back."

"I will," she assured him, then hung up.

"So, what did he say?" Logan asked as she tucked the phone into her jacket.

"That you're hired."

"Excellent." He pushed off the wall. "And what else?"

"What makes you think there was something else?"

"I just know."

Alex hoped super hearing wasn't part of his genetic profile. Or mind reading. She swallowed hard.

"He told me to be careful because assassins cannot be trusted."

"Sound advice," he agreed. "Assassins cannot be trusted."

"Indeed."

"But I won't betray you, Alex."

"You'd better not. I have no problem stapling you to the wall."

She followed him through a set of double doors. The words 'Hell on Earth' were spray-painted in glittery pink letters across them. As they passed into an open hall, Alex realized she hadn't, in fact, been chained up in the basement but just a mostly windowless room. More graffiti covered the walls: a lot of supernatural motifs, as well as some skulls and crossbones, a few roses, and a duck procession that would have belonged better on a preschool wall.

A shiny red door waited at the other end of the cavernous room. A painted dragon covered most of that wall. Red and orange flames spilled out of its mouth. Steam rose from the lake. Houses, trees, and people had caught on fire. The artist had spent a lot of time painting the tortured looks on their faces. They looked almost lifelike.

"That's Radiance's work there," Logan said. "He goes all around Europe, painting scenes like this. Dragons killing humans. Mages killing humans. Vampires killing humans. Do you sense a pattern?"

She nodded. Most humans revered magic; they even thought that if they were just lucky enough, they'd someday gain the power of magic too. The Magic Council had done an excellent job of propagating that myth. Of course it didn't work that way, but this little lie kept the majority of the human population from turning against them. Funny how those things worked.

But then there were those humans who feared and hated supernaturals, no matter what. Obviously, Radiance was firmly in this category and believed everyone else should join him at Camp Hate.

"You chained me up inside the Rote Fabrik?" Alex said as they stepped outside.

She looked up at the layers of red bricks that made up the former factory. There were always a bunch of musical and cultural events going on in some part or another of the large building, most of them supernatural.

Dust, a fairy bar located there, was probably the most famous. A couple weeks ago, Alex had visited it with Marek while tracking down a herd of lost unicorns. How could anyone lose a herd of two dozen unicorns? The answer was ancient teleportation glyphs, forgotten magic that even Marek hadn't known about. They'd learned about it the hard way: by being teleported into the lake, where they'd had to fight free of a sea monster living there. Fun times.

"Sure. Why not? The walls are stable and no one even

blinks if you carry chains in there."

"That is really disturbing. Just so you know."

"Carrying in chains?"

"That too," she agreed. "Where are we going?"

"Just to a little place I know nearby."

"For information on the Orbs?"

"Yes."

Logan wasn't lying when he said his 'little place' was nearby. They hadn't been walking for more than a few minutes when he stopped in front of a cute two-story house. It had a slanted red roof and wood details framed around the windows and crisscrossed along the front face. A perfect Swiss chalet—in the city. On the top level balcony, two fairies lay on reclining lawn chairs, bathing in the morning light. Below them, right beside the front door, hung a wooden sign that read 'Honor Among Thieves' in a swirly cursive script.

"I don't like the look of that," Alex said.

"The fairies' sign?"

"The name of this establishment."

"You wanted to figure out who's after the Orbs. There's no better place to start than at a bar full of professional thieves."

"Professional thieves. It sounds better than pickpockets."

"These are the best in the business, Alex," he told her. "They won't take on a job worth less than six figures, which generally means something supernatural. If anyone knows who's after the Orbs, these fellows will."

"Ok." She rolled back her head, stretching out the stiffness. A stream of pops scraped across her neck. "Damn it, Logan. I'm stiff all over from sleeping in those stupid chains. I'm going to have to do yoga for at least an hour when I get home tonight."

His eyes lit up. "Can I watch?"

"No, you may not."

"Participate?"

"Absolutely not," she said, brushing past him to enter the building.

The interior was surprisingly well-lit for a bar full of scoundrels. An assortment of tasteful hanging lamps dangled from the ceiling: orange and red frosted glass cylinders, pale blue cubes, and a few yellow mesh boards that resembled kites sewn together in triplet bundles. The floor was made of glossy red tiles, which blended beautifully with the warm tones of the cherrywood bar and the other furniture in the room.

There were only eight people in the room, which was eight more people than you'd see in any other bar in the city at this early hour. A blue-haired fairy with enormous breasts and a tiny waist stood beside the bar, wiping down the tabletop in sensual strokes. When she saw Logan, she winked, then turned so he could have a better view of her ass as she caressed the bar with that silly pink dishtowel.

A pair of male mages sat at a nearby table, sipping nectar and munching on peanuts. They were bent over a large sheet of paper spread out between them, but every so often, one of them would steal a look at the Blue Fairy. Bah, men.

A few tables over, a pair of fairies dressed like they were ready to raid an Egyptian tomb were flipping through pictures on a phone screen. One of them, who looked like the male equivalent of the Blue Fairy, shot the mages an icy glare. He must have been her brother. His female companion wore twin pink braids beneath her sable fedora.

But not all the thieves here were supernatural. Three

human men stood in front of a cork board tacked full of jobs. One of them pointed at a square card with a crimson border.

"A job from the vampires," Logan told her. "The jobs are all color-coded. Crimson for vampires, gold for mages, green for humans, blue for fairies, and silver for the otherworldly."

"The otherworldly? What could ghosts and phantoms possibly want to steal?"

"Usually things that were once theirs, back when they were alive, but they've lost track of since. Sometimes, they just want to steal from people living in their former houses. Or from another otherworldly they despise."

"What a bizarre way to spend eternity," she said. "Do you think whoever wants the Orbs put up a notice here? There was one up at Impulse."

"Yes, a notice with a black border." He walked toward the wall with the board. "Black means whoever is paying wants to remain anonymous."

"Is that a common color?"

"Not really. Often enough people who want something stolen also want the victim to know who it was that stole from them. It's all part of the game."

"What game?"

"The game for power," he replied. "Black borders are a lot more common on the assassin boards."

"There are assassin boards?"

"Of course."

"Where would I find one?"

"You don't. They're secret."

Too bad. Alex could prevent a lot more vicious killings if she knew they were coming. Then again, maybe it was for the best. She'd probably find herself on that board. She'd made her share of enemies since coming to Zurich. Last night, one of them had even tried to poison her. How long would it be before someone else made a move on her?

"Slayer," one of the human thieves said as she and Logan stopped in front of the board.

"Brigand." Logan returned the manly nod, then pointed at the Orbs notice. "Say, have you heard anything about this job?"

"Two million," the thief read, letting out a low whistle. "That's a pretty prize there. But I hear two of the Orbs have already been stolen. A bit late to the game this time, aren't you, Slayer?"

His companions snickered. Logan stared at them until their chortles dissolved into coughs.

"Do you know who put up the reward?" he asked.

Brigand looked at the others, who both shook their heads. "No."

Not one of them looked like they gave a hoot who it was either. They all looked scared of Logan, though.

"So are you going after those Orbs yourself, Slayer?" one of them asked.

Logan flashed the thief a deadly smile. "Why, yes I am."

The thief gave him a jerky nod, then retreated to the bar. Brigand cleared his throat.

"Ok," Alex said slowly, her words cutting through the uncomfortable silence like a dull butcher knife. "Let's try asking the other—"

Logan slammed her against the wall. A ball of silver lightning sizzled past, narrowly missing them. Logan spun around, launching two knives across the room as he turned. The two mages lashed out with whips of lightning magic, flicking the knives away.

"Are you all right?" Logan asked Alex.

"Fine." She drew her sword. "Let's take these bozos down."

CHAPTER EIGHT

Magic Breaker

DESPITE THEIR FLASHY opening, the mage brothers didn't put up much of a fight. Alex and Logan had them pinned to the notice board within the first minute. It was what happened next that was the problem.

The human thieves charged as one at Logan, tackling him to the floor. And while Alex was trying to get them off of him, the mages broke free and summoned a thunderstorm inside the bar.

"Idiots," Alex muttered, looking up at the dark storm clouds swirling against the ceiling.

Glass shattered, the fuse popped, and every single light in the room went out. Overhead, pink and purple lightning snapped and sizzled over the constant hum of the clouds, casting the room in an eerie magical light. Keeping low, Alex crept toward the mages, who had created a protective bubble of sparkling silver energy around themselves. It sure looked pretty, but more importantly it looked potent enough to knock out most supernaturals on contact.

It was a good thing Alex wasn't most supernaturals.

"Not another step, assassin!" one of the mages shouted

over the storm.

Logan ducked, and the blast of lightning meant for him crackled against the tabletop and bounced up to the ceiling. The other mage launched a fireball. The table Logan was using as a barrier burst into flames.

A nearby glass candle cover exploded. A splattering of tiny—and a few not-so-tiny—shards sank through Alex's jacket into her arm. Hot fire burned from the wounds, flooding her body. She swore under her breath, then quickly blocked out the pain. There was no time for first aid now. She had a duo of mages to fry.

Alex inched toward the shiny barrier, reaching out with her hands. There were times when being an abomination came in handy, and this was one of them. No one could break magic like a Dragon Born. She slid her fingertips across the invisible film outside the barrier, an elastic layer that held the magic together.

"And here's a nice April blizzard for you!" one of the mages shouted at Logan.

Alex pushed their raving threats out of her head and focused on the barrier. Her finger caught on a loose edge and she pulled. Harder and harder, she tugged on the unraveling thread. The barrier was weakening, its tautness dissolving into melting jelly. Close enough. She punched her fist through the outer rim. The barrier shook—then all the mages' spells popped and came gushing down, dissolving into smoky wisps before they could hit the ground.

Their magic broken, the mages fainted like the lightweights they were. Alex rose and looked over the scene of burning tables and scorched walls. Cracked glass shifted beneath her boots as she joined Logan beside the bar.

Two of the human thieves lay unconscious at his feet,

ropes binding their ankles and wrists. The third man was unconscious too, and from the looks of the nasty bump on his head, he wouldn't be waking up anytime soon. Logan pulled out another pair of ropes and made quick work of him.

"Forgot your chains?" Alex asked him.

His lip twitched, but he didn't smile. "I have something better in mind."

That 'something better' was stringing all five napping thieves from the ceiling to replace the lamps they'd broken. They looked more like hanging meat at the butcher's shop than lights, especially dangling upside down from their ankle bindings. Logan sure knew how to make a statement.

Speaking of the assassin, he was lying reclined on a sofa against the wall, his head in the Blue Fairy's lap. Ostensibly, she was tending to his wounds—he had a nasty cut on his lip—but in reality, she just wanted an excuse to make bedroom eyes at him while pushing her cleavage in his face. There wasn't enough fabric in her shirt to sew together a pair of panties.

"Slayer, you fought so valiantly," she cooed, patting the corner of a wet towel to his lip. "But my poor bar. It's absolutely ruined."

The noise from the fight had caught the attention of the two sunbathing fairies from the upstairs balcony; they'd come down for drinks. They gave Blue sympathetic looks.

"Those misfits will pay for the damages. I'll make sure of it," he assured her.

"Oh, I know you will." She batted her magically-extended eyelashes at him. "You are such an honorable man. And so strong," she added, giving his bicep a sensual stroke.

Alex tried not to gag, but a dry cough escaped her lips.

The Blue Fairy threw a dismissive look over her shoulder. "Say, where did you find your new apprentice, Slayer?"

Alex folded her arms across her chest and glared at the blue strumpet.

"You mean Alex?" Logan said, sitting up. "She's not my apprentice. She's a mercenary working for Gaelyn."

"Mercenary," the fairy repeated, her nose bunching up like she didn't care for the smell of the word. "That certainly explains things." She smirked at Alex. "Especially the questionable fashion sense."

Alex wanted to punch her in her pretty little face.

"But we can't really blame her, I suppose. If I spent most of my time hacking apart monsters… No, who am I kidding?" She let out a breathy giggle. "I'd still do it in style."

Yeah, that would last long. Basically, up until her stilettos got stuck in a pile of goo, and the monster who'd made it munched her down for dinner.

"Do you know anything about what Drake has been up to lately?" Logan said quickly, shaking his head.

The movement was so subtle that she almost missed it. She didn't miss the stern gleam in his eyes, though. The assassin, the man who *killed* people for a living, was reminding her to behave herself. Like she would punch the snooty fairy, even though Blue totally deserved it. Alex could control herself for five minutes.

"Drake? The vampire elf? Yeah, he was in yesterday morning. Said he had a big job, then would head over to the range afterwards to practice," Blue Fairy told him.

"Range?"

"The shooting range, of course. He's competing in the supernatural tournament this afternoon."

"Right, Supernatural Steel," he said. "I'd forgotten all about it."

"Does that mean you're not competing?"

"I don't think so."

"Shame." She pushed out her thick, pouty lips. "I do like watching you…work."

"I'll try to make an appearance." Logan stood up. "Thanks for your help. And if any of them give you trouble…" He looked up at the dangling thieves. "…let me know."

"You know I will." From the look in her eyes, she was already thinking up an excuse to call Logan here.

Whatever. None of your business, she told herself.

That's right, she agreed…uh, with herself.

Trying not to think about how crazy that was, Alex turned and followed Logan outside.

CHAPTER NINE
House of Chocolate

THEY WALKED BACK to the Rote Fabrik. Logan had parked his car around the back, close to the lake. And, yeah, it was a glossy black Maserati. The assassin business must have been booming.

"So, what kind of, um, assignments do you take?" Alex asked him as she got into his car.

He started the engine. "You mean, what sort of people do I kill?"

"Yes."

"Only bad people, sweetheart."

"Really?"

"No." He slid the car smoothly into traffic—'traffic' being the three cars driving on the street at this time of day. "I won't kill complete innocents. They aren't worth much money anyway."

"That's not funny."

"I wasn't trying to be. My targets are all high-profile: warlords, monsters, corrupt businessman. They wouldn't have such a high price on their heads if they hadn't done something to earn it. They've all done a lot of bad things, though I'd be lying if I said they'd done only bad. No one is one hundred percent evil. Not even the monsters you kill."

"We are not the same."

"Yes. We are very much the same, Alex. Did you ask the last vampire you killed what his life was like before magic stripped away his humanity? Or chat with the last dark pony about her children?"

"They're monsters," she said.

"We're *all* monsters," he countered. "The only difference is that some of us have already admitted that to ourselves."

"You're awfully philosophical for an assassin."

"Yes." He looked at her. "I suppose I am."

She turned her eyes away from him. The world had labeled her kind abominations, which was just a fancy word for monster. If the Magic Council offered him a contract to kill the last Dragon Born, would he accept? Probably. He didn't seem to have a problem killing monsters for profit.

Neither did she. He was right. If the situation were different—if she hadn't been Dragon Born herself—she'd have believed the propaganda too. She'd have hunted down innocent mages whose only crime was to be born a bit different. And she'd have profited from it too.

"I thought we were going to the tournament," she said as he continued to follow the street down the lake.

"It doesn't start until this afternoon. I thought we'd have something to eat first."

"Good idea." Her stomach growled, letting its wishes be heard. "Some crazy person locked me up in chains, so I didn't get breakfast."

"I was going to offer you something, but then you attacked me."

"You had that coming," she told him. "So what sort of

something were you going to offer me?"

"Granola."

"Yuck. Try my sister. She loves granola. I hate it."

"I also had a chocolate croissant."

"Better."

"And a glass of freshly squeezed orange juice."

"Mmm. I'll consider forgiving you. Someday. Where are these delicious treats?"

"Some vagrant must have stolen them while you were busy attacking me. When I went back to the room I'd left them in, they were gone. I have security cameras set up all around that hall. As soon as all this is over, I'm going to look through the footage and find out who it was."

The dark look in his eyes sent goosebumps prickling across her skin.

"Or you could just leave it be," she said. "The loss of a breakfast tray is hardly going to send you to the poorhouse."

"It's not about the money. It's that someone stole something *from me.*"

She snorted. "Proud much?"

"I have a reputation to uphold. No client will be interested in hiring the great Slayer when word gets out that some miscreant stole his croissant."

"Did anyone ever tell you how weird it is to talk about yourself in the third person?"

"No." A wicked smile slid up his lips. "Paranormal Vigilante. Or was that Black Plague?"

"The name 'Black Plague' is tons scarier than 'Slayer'. Admit it."

"I will do no such thing."

"Come on. The Black Plague would totally slay the Slayer."

"You realize you're now speaking about yourself in the third person."

"And?" she said. "I never said I wasn't weird."

His low chuckle blended with the hum of the engine as he turned into the lot and parked. Alex jumped out of the car, practically drooling from the olfactory overload of cakes, cookies, chocolates, and other tasty sweets. He'd brought them to Madam Meringue's House of Chocolate.

Madam Meringue was a mage with an almost divine ability to mix potions—or in this case, chocolate. She was the undisputed champion of Magical Sciences. Every magic company wanted to hire her. Every magic university had tried to recruit her. Even the Magic Council had made her a prestigious offer. She'd turned them all down.

When the supernaturals had started flocking to Zurich, Madam Meringue had found herself a nice lakeside chocolate factory to buy. They hadn't wanted to sell, but she'd made them an offer they couldn't refuse. She was convinced that, with a little touch of magic, she could make the world's best chocolate. It hadn't taken long for the world to agree.

Now, Madam Meringue's House of Chocolate was the name for top-of-the-line chocolate. She had magic-kissed chocolate for the human masses, but it was her specialty line that attracted the supernaturals in droves.

"This is so amazing," Alex said, pulling out her phone. "Epic even." She snapped a photo of the huge dragon-shaped balloon bobbing beside the entrance.

Logan watched her with perplexed amusement. "I had no idea you were such a fan."

"I'm always a fan of chocolate. Especially good chocolate." She spotted a life-sized unicorn balloon with 'Madam Meringue's House of Chocolate' printed on the side. "And most especially chocolate for breakfast. Or lunch." Click. "But these photos aren't for me. They're for my brother. He's the Madam Meringue fan." She took a shot of the enormous chocolate ball balloon. "He's studying Magical Sciences at SFUMAS."

"Snafu?"

"Funny."

She snapped a shot of him standing under the goofy chocolate ball. If he annoyed her too much, she might decide to post it on the internet later. Maybe even as a comment to his profile on the Assassins List website. 'Death by chocolate. Deadly assassin Slayer will kill you with a taste.' Yeah, that should send the right kind of traffic his way.

"SFUMAS," Alex repeated. "San Francisco University of Magical Arts and Sciences. Riley is a whizz at the Magical Sciences, and Madam Meringue is his hero. He will be positively stoked when I show him these photos. Wait, a second." She handed Logan her phone. "Here, get a photo of me next to the dragon. Otherwise, he'll never believe I was actually here."

Logan shook his head in disbelief but snapped the shot anyway. "This proves nothing. You could have just photoshopped yourself in."

"That requires a subtlety Riley knows I do not possess. Why do you think I carry around a sword? I'm blunt, and I like fast results."

"You said it, not I."

Alex took the phone back and tucked it into her leather jacket. She was really starting to question if the all-leather ensemble was such a great idea after all. Sure, she looked badass, but she was starting to sweat. The sun was nearly overhead, so it would only get worse from here on out. Of course, she usually didn't wear such things during the day. When she'd put it on and gone out last night, she hadn't done so with the intention of getting drugged and abducted.

"Has anyone ever looked into why a Magical Sciences 'whizz' has two sisters who claim to be magic duds?" Logan asked.

"What's your point?"

"It doesn't add up is my point. Magic runs in families."

"But not everyone in a magic family is equally powerful. And sometimes there's a member or two without any magic whatsoever. In fact, if we are to believe the Magic Council, there are members of non-magic families who suddenly sprout magic."

"You don't believe that nonsense, and neither do I," he told her. "Most of what the Magic Council says is complete drivel, nothing but sugar-coated lies to placate the masses."

"Sera and I don't have any magic," Alex said, keeping her breathing normal and her heartbeat steady. A change in either was a telltale sign every assassin would know to look for when trying to sniff out a lie. And she was lying through her teeth right now. "When we were in school, we were tested like everyone else. I'm not pretending to be a magic dud; that was their assessment."

"You dissolved iron chains." He counted out one finger. "You shattered a magic barrier back in the fairy bar." He paused on the second finger, frowning. "I'm still not sure how you did that. I've never seen anything like it before."

"There was a hole in the barrier."

"I'm sure. There's always a hole, isn't there? How convenient." He flipped open the third finger. "And lastly, you don't fight like a human. You can make up whatever wild stories about chemical agents and holes about the other two, but this one you cannot explain. I've fought a lot of people—human and supernatural. And you are not human, sweetheart. Not by a long shot."

"You don't fight like a human either, Mr. Super Soldier."

"I told you what I am."

"Genetically engineered? Sounds like a 'wild story' to me."

"You can believe whatever you want. It's the truth."

"Right back at you."

He sighed. "You are an impossible woman. There's no point in arguing with you."

She folded her arms across her chest and gave him a triumphant grin. "Precisely."

"Let's just grab something to eat while we have the chance. The tournament will be starting soon," he said, opening the door for her.

"What a fantastic idea," she replied and walked through it—even though it probably wasn't a good idea to turn her back to an assassin.

Whatever. If he'd wanted to kill her, he would have done it already. Like back when she'd been unconscious and in chains. But he hadn't. They were working together now, and she'd just have to trust him. For now. Besides, the perfume of a million magical flavors of chocolate was drawing her forward.

Inside, chocolate filled the shelves of the shop—bars, balls, bunnies and a few other animals—but that's not what caught Alex's attention. She headed straight for the cafe. With a dozen chairs around a smattering of tables and only half as many stools at the bar, it wasn't big. It didn't matter. The assortment of cakes and cookies behind the glass display counter spoke for itself. This place was heaven on earth.

Alex ordered a cake sampler plate, a cookie sandwich with cream filling, and a glass of freshly squeezed orange juice. Then she took a seat at one of the tables and spread out her treasure. Logan joined her, carrying nothing.

"Afraid someone will try to poison your food?" she asked, smirking.

"In my profession, that is a distinct possibility," he replied. "But no, I'm simply not hungry. I ate already."

"Then why are we here?"

"Because I knew you were hungry. And you seemed like someone who would appreciate chocolate for breakfast," he said, watching her as she assaulted the cookie.

Her mouth busy appreciating the delightful marriage of cookie and magic, Alex grunted her approval.

"It appears I was right. Considering your obvious love of chocolate, I'm surprised you haven't come here yet."

"I've only been here two months." Alex skewered a cheesecake cube with her fork. "And I've been busy making the city safe from monsters. Did you know that the number of monsters in Zurich has more than tripled in the last two months?"

"Yes. I've been here a bit longer than you. It used to be warlords and corrupt mage bankers seeking haven, but the monsters have run most of them out of the area. Business has been bad."

She took a sip of the juice. It was almost as good as a magic smoothie. "How could business possibly be bad? You are an assassin. There's no shortage of things to kill in the city. What difference does it make to you whether your target is a warlord or a monster?"

"The payment makes a hell of a difference to me. A dead warlord is worth several million. A dead monster isn't worth more than a few hundred."

"Sure. That's where sheer numbers work in your favor." She pointed her fork at him. "A hundred dead monsters isn't a bad payout. Good luck rounding up a hundred warlords."

"And how long does it take you to kill those hundred monsters? A few hours?"

"Depends."

"Why spend a few hours mucking around in monster guts when I can make a single clean kill in a fraction of that time?"

"And what about all the kills you have to make on your way to your mark?"

"Most of them can be avoided. Including the monsters," he said. "But you, Alex, can't avoid the messy kills on the way to the job. Those messy kills *are* the job."

"I guess we'll just have to agree to disagree," she replied. Served her right for trying to argue logistics with an assassin. Sampling the piece of fudge on her plate was far more productive. "So, did you know that while the number of monsters in Zurich has tripled in the last two months, the number of supernatural hybrids has increased tenfold during the same timeframe?"

"I do remember reading that in Supernatural Times."

"I wonder where they're all coming from. Hybrids don't just pop up out of nowhere."

"Someone is making them," he said.

"Really?"

"Of course. It's only logical."

"I wonder who it is."

He gave her a hard look. "Someone you should not try to find."

"I wasn't—"

"You were. I saw that spark in your eyes. It's the one you get right before you're about to do something reckless. Anyone who has the magic to create supernatural hybrids must be very powerful. And going after someone that powerful is reckless."

"You and Marek should be best friends," she muttered.

"The dragon summoner?" His mouth drew into a hard line. "He's…flamboyant."

"He most certainly is." Alex snickered. "Ok, so maybe you two don't see eye-to-eye on fashion. But you both are operating under the misconception that I am reckless. I'm *not* reckless."

He snatched up her hand from the table, turning her arm until he could see the shredded leather at the shoulder. "Thought I wouldn't see this, did you?"

"That wasn't me being reckless." She pulled her arm free. "It was a pair of mages being crazy."

"You shouldn't have been in that bar in the first place. It's full of criminals."

"*You* brought me to that bar."

"You shouldn't be hanging around me either. I'm an assassin."

Alex felt her jaw pop. "You're the one who wanted to work with me," she reminded him.

"Yes, and I still do. But that doesn't mean hanging around me isn't reckless of you."

"You sure have an odd way of convincing me to work with you."

"There's no need to convince you of anything. I'm already working with you." His eyes drifted to the shoulder she was rubbing. "Are you seriously hurt?"

"No, it's ok. Just a bit sore. I dealt with the wounds after the fight." She smirked at him. "Blue didn't offer to pat my skin with a wet towel."

"Blue?"

"The fairy who was popping out of that piece of lingerie she thought was a dress."

"I see."

"She had eyes only for you."

"Jealous?"

Yes. "No, she's not my type."

He leaned across the table. "And what is your type?"

Apparently, assassins. No, not assassins. Definitely not assassins. Because that really would be reckless.

"Alex?" he asked, leaning in further. His hand caressed her cheek, feather-soft, brushing back her hair. It slid across her neck...

She clenched up as he scraped across the vampire bite.

"What's this?" Logan asked, looking it over. "It looks like someone bit you."

"Someone did. A vampire elf. I thought you were watching the fight."

"I had to run before the end of it," he said. "It doesn't look that bad." He pulled back far enough to look her in the eye. "Should I be worried that you'll turn into a vampire and eat me up?"

She shrugged. "If that was going to happen, I would have already changed into a vampire."

"You're immune to vampire venom?"

"Gaelyn thinks I've built up a resistance to it from the last time I was bitten."

"You've been bitten before?"

"Just a nip."

He looked as surprised as an assassin could be—which was to say his eyebrows might have lifted a tad. "So, you're immune to vampire venom. And to the poison Hugh tried on you last night. You can dissolve iron chains," he tallied off. "What are you?"

"I'm just a mercenary who fights monsters. That's all you need to know."

She hoped he didn't know enough about magical history to add it all up and figure out she was Dragon Born. The magic-breaking was probably a dead giveaway; there weren't too many Magic Breakers, and most of them were really underpowered. Alex didn't know much about the Dragon Born, except that in addition to sniffing out magic, her kind was supposed to have had the power to break any spell.

Her sister Sera thought the Dragon Born didn't have much to do with dragons, but Alex wasn't too sure. They did know that the Dragon Born mages had gotten their name from the unique circumstance of their birth: like dragons, they were two souls born into one body and later separated by magic. They'd once been the most powerful mages in the world, thanks to an unusual effect of the separation spell. According to ancient lore, when the two souls were split each into their own body, their magic multiplied instead of divided. Each new mage had the power of two. Just like the dragons.

So if the Dragon Born were born like dragons, couldn't they also share other things in common with them?

It was too bad there weren't any dragons left to ask. They'd died out long ago. There weren't any Dragon Born left either because the Magic Council had declared them abominations and hunted them to near extinction. As far as Alex knew, she and Sera were the only ones in the world. Though it's not like any other Dragon Born would be quick to speak up. To do so would mean their death.

"You are a lot more than 'just a mercenary who fights

monsters'," Logan said. "That much is certain."

CHAPTER TEN

Supernatural Steel

THERE WEREN'T MANY places open for business in Zurich on a Sunday, but the things you could count on were train stations, bars, and shooting areas.

Supernatural Steel, the citywide shooting tournament for Zurich's magic population, was held every year at the Glass Dome. Large enough to hold a soccer field, the dome was made of UV-blocking glass, an important consideration when a sizable fraction of the participant pool was sunlight averse.

Logan parked in a spot spray-painted with the picture of a pair of crossed daggers over a skull. Alex didn't know what the symbol meant—and she probably didn't want to. It must have had something to do with being an assassin. One thing was perfectly clear, though: if a regular joe tried to park in a space like that, the parking police would be the least of their worries.

Alex and Logan followed the stone path from the parking lot to the entrance hall. Inside the building, Rustic Charm had teamed up with Modern Elegance to dance the do-si-do of interior decorating. The blended look worked surprisingly well. The floors were made of elegant beige tiles, the ceiling dripped with strands of tiny magic lamps, and the reception desk looked like a log from an ancient tree.

Three fairies with brilliant smiles and enormous 'volunteer' badges sat behind the desk. Another five people —some fairies, some mages—hurried back and forth in the background, fetching manila folders and participant bags. On the wall behind them hung paintings of supernatural scenes that were obviously supposed to be idyllic. Vampire cowboys. Fairy acrobats. Ghost professors. Mage warriors.

Logan cut to the front of the very long line, eliciting a few angry protests from the waiting supernaturals. Most of them grew quiet as soon as they saw it was Slayer cutting them; the sight of the Black Plague and her big sword silenced the rest. A few of them shuffled to the back of the line. The looks on their faces said they wanted to be as far as supernaturally possible from Alex and Logan.

"Well, aren't we a regular crowd-killing duo," she whispered to him.

Logan looked over his shoulder, his green eyes assessing the scene. "It makes things simpler."

"Like line cutting?"

"For instance." He looked at the purple-pigtailed fairy sitting behind the counter. "We'd like to enter the tournament."

The fairy gaped at him for a second before remembering to paste on her dazzling smile. "Of course. Slayer, right? And Black Plague?"

"That's Paranormal Vigilante," Alex muttered.

The fairy breezed right past the interruption, her glittery nails flicking through the stapled list of participants. "Are you registered?"

"No, how about you take care of that now," Logan said.

She opened her mouth to protest, then must have thought better of it. "Ok." She pulled out a sheet of paper and a pencil with a unicorn eraser on the end. "Which division? We have Fairy, Mage, Vampire, and the Wild Card group for humans."

It made sense. For obvious reasons, there was no otherworldly division.

"Two wild cards," Logan told her.

"Slayer." She began to write on the paper in a long, loopy script. "And Black Plague."

"Paranormal Vigilante."

The fairy continued to write. "The Wild Card qualifying rounds start in twenty-five minutes. Please go through the double doors and wait in the Ballista Room with the other Wild Card competitors until your names are called."

"Where are the vampires waiting? And the fairies?" Logan asked her.

The fairy volunteer dropped her pencil. "Assassinations are strictly prohibited on the premises."

"I'm not going to assassinate anyone," Logan said.

No, he's just going to show the thief his knives, Alex thought.

"Sorry, I can't help you." The fairy handed them their bags, waved the next person in line up to the counter.

"I don't think she believed you," Alex muttered as they pushed through the double doors that led into the back.

"So it would appear."

He sped up to close the distance to a group of gabbing fairies with rifles and crossbows swung over their shoulders. They'd almost have looked tough—if not for the knee-highs and short schoolgirl skirts. The huge polkadot butterfly bows in their hair weren't doing their lethal image any favors either.

"Did you bring your gun?" Logan asked Alex.

"Gun? What gun? I don't even own one."

"Crossbow?"

"No."

"Do you have any form of long distance weapon?"

Alex thought about that for a moment. "That depends. Will they let me throw my knives?"

"No."

"My sword?"

"No."

"Then this could prove to be problematic. Just how long are we going to let this little charade play out?"

"As long as it takes to find Drake and ask him some questions about the Orbs."

Logan scanned the room the schoolgirls they'd been following had just entered. There were about two dozen fairies inside of various types, including a few elves—but no vampire elves.

"That might take awhile," she said. "We're not actually going to participate in the tournament, are we?"

"No. But you need to look like you're ready to participate."

"Ok." She showed him her sweetest smile. "Give me a gun to carry around."

"On second thought, I'll look ready for the both of us."

"Spoilsport."

A vampire passed between them, pausing in the doorway to the room. He gave the fairies a superior sneer, then puffed out his chest, expelled a grunt worthy of a minotaur, and turned to leave. Logan trailed him.

"We're about to step into a room full of vampires who

like to shoot things for fun," Alex whispered, walking beside him. "Are you sure you don't want to give me a gun? I promise not to shoot you in the back until after the fight."

He gave her a cool look. "Do you ever stop joking?"

"No. It helps calm my nerves."

"Try meditation."

"In the middle of a fight?"

"No. At home, now and then."

"I'm not very good at sitting still and doing nothing," she said. "I do yoga, though."

"I remember." His coolness evaporated, the look in his eyes burning the frost away. "And I'm still waiting for my invitation."

"To work out with me?" She poked her finger at his chest, and it hit solid muscle. Ouch. "You couldn't keep up with me, assassin."

"Cute, Alex. Very cute. I was training back when you still didn't even know what a sword was."

"Unless you're a lot older than you look, I very much doubt that," she replied. "I always knew what a sword was. My father put one in my hand as soon as I could walk. And he taught me how to use it."

"That explains a few things."

"How crazy I am?"

"How well you fight," he said. "Why did he teach you to fight?"

"Because the world is a scary place, full of monsters. He wanted to make sure we had the skills to keep ourselves safe. And it was a good thing he did."

"What happened?"

"When Sera and I were sixteen, an assassin killed our dad." *Except he was really after us. Because, you know, we're abominations.* "We had to take care of ourselves after that.

And our little brother too."

"That's why you became a monster-hunting mercenary."

"Yes. It paid better than anything else we could get."

"Though not as much as if you had a magic rating."

"That's how it works, yes. Sera and I are on the bottom rung of the pay scale for monster-hunting mercenaries. The money wasn't great, but it was enough."

"Until Gaelyn hired you."

She nodded. "He pays…well, there really are no words for that. Gaelyn hired me through my guild Mayhem, so the guild still gets their pretty sizable cut. But it's more money than I've ever seen before in my life."

"I do like your new boots."

"So do I. And the jacket. I even bought myself a bracelet." She lifted her hand and jiggled it; the silver strands of tiny gemstones slipped out from under her sleeve and brushed across her wrist.

"I saw." He caught her hand, brushing a finger across the bracelet. "It looks good on you. Though I would have gone for something with real diamonds."

"I'll remember that if I ever decide to enter the assassin business," she said drily.

"If you ever enter the assassin business," he replied, his fingertips dancing lightly across her hand. "I want to have the chance to make you an offer?"

"What kind of offer?"

"To work for me."

"I thought you worked alone."

"I do," he told her. "But for someone with your rare abilities, I'd make an exception. Just imagine what the two of us could do together."

Imagine what they could do together? Probably a lot of things that didn't have much to do with assassinating. Or wearing clothes…

"Alex?"

She gave her dirty mind a mental slap. "Yes?"

"We've found the vampire waiting room."

The vampire they'd been trailing had gone through a door with a bright red frame. How fitting.

"How do you want to do this?" she asked Logan. "Should I go take a peek to see if the jerk who chowed down on my neck is in there?"

"We'll go together." He moved beside her. "Get your knives ready, just in case. You know how vampires are."

Yep, she knew. Vampires were moody beasts. Whether shape-shifting, demon-possessed, or just plain old crazy common vampires—they liked to get themselves worked up into a fit. The first two breeds piled on some extra drama while they were at it. The third kind cut to the chase and went straight for the jugular.

"Ok." Alex slid a knife down to the tip of each jacket sleeve, where she'd be able to hurl them quickly if the need arose. "Let's do this."

Side-by-side, they stepped into the doorway. Alex scanned the room, finding Drake immediately. But he wasn't alone. He stood in a sea of big and buff vampires, every single one of their eyes glowing with demon-charged power.

CHAPTER ELEVEN
Vampire Gunner

"DRAKE," SAID THE biggest of the vampire muscle men.

From the way the rest of the vampires were looking at him, he was the clear leader of the pack. His body was bathed in leather, his skin aglow with magic aftershave. Yeah, that's right. Demon vampires shaved, most of them at least twice a day. The demon powering their strength and speed also shot their hair growth into overdrive. Alex often wondered if they minded that little side effect.

Drake's weird hybrid magic went haywire. It split and sizzled like a torn power line. "Wait, Gunner. Please. I need more time."

Gunner the vampire gunner? Either his parents had the gift of foresight, or Gunner was really bad at picking stage names.

"Time's up. We want our money now."

"So this is a shakedown?" the vampire elf said, his magic letting out an uneven belch. It smelled like junkyard parts and day-old sweat—certainly nothing like the usual flowery aroma of the fairies.

"It will become a beatdown if you don't show us our

money fast, you sniveling halfbreed."

"It's not here." As Gunner pulled back his fist, Drake winced. "Wait! I'll have it soon."

"We've heard that before. Haven't we, boys?" Gunner asked his gang.

All the men nodded—and the two female vampires too.

"Soon," Drake said quickly. "Real soon. I'm just waiting to get paid for those Orbs."

"You stole the Fairy and Vampire Orbs?"

"With my group, yes."

Gunner chuckled. "You must have a death wish. The Vampire Covenant is out for blood. They insist that they will find whoever is responsible for stealing the Blood Orb. And if they don't find you, Gaelyn's supernatural exterminator will. The Paranormal Vigilante, wasn't it?"

"People are calling her the Black Plague," one of the female vampires told him.

"The Paranormal Vigilante won't be a problem. At least not for long," Drake said smugly. "I bit her. She'll either die or transform. Whatever the case may be, she's out of the picture."

"A scrawny weakling like you took down the infamous Paranormal Vigilante?" the vampire with the mohawk asked in pure disbelief.

"Yes." Drake grinned, the little liar.

"I hope she turns," another vampire said. Tattoos covered every inch of skin on both his arms. "That Vigilante is hot."

"I'd love to see what's under all that leather she wears," added Mohawk.

Ew. And double ew. Alex resisted the urge to inform them that they weren't her type. First of all, she preferred living men. And secondly, those demonic eyes were just creepy.

"Don't do it," Logan whispered to her.

"Do what?"

"You know what. I saw your hand reach toward your sword."

"My fingers were stiff. I was just stretching them out."

"Sure you were." Though his aura rippled with amusement, his face maintained its granite mask. "The vampires haven't noticed us yet. Let's not do anything reckless."

Alex made sure he was looking at her before giving her eyes a long, slow roll. As she returned her attention to the vampires, she could have sworn she heard him chuckle. Gunner's gang was still discussing her. Half of the vampires were verbally undressing her. The other half of them were debating how best to kill a vigilante.

In other words, she hadn't missed a thing.

"Ok, settle down, guys," Gunner said, interrupting a particularly vile vampire who was talking about his previous vigilante conquests—both on the battlefield and in the bedroom. "We need to concentrate on the matter at hand." His white-iron gaze shifted to Drake.

The vampire elf squeaked in alarm. "A week. Give me a week."

"Well," Gunner said with a lazy yawn. "I just sipped from a tasty fairy this afternoon, so I'm feeling generous. You have one day to bring me my money."

"Ok," Drake replied, slouching in defeat.

Gunner gave him a rough slap on the back, then walked off to look after his weapons. The other demon vampires followed. Drake watched them put their guns together with almost morbid fascination. Or maybe that was his deer-in-headlights look. His eyes did a nervous sweep of the room, freezing when they fell on Alex and Logan standing in the hall.

"Ah, looks like your vigilante is alive after all," Gunner commented, giving Alex a playful wink.

"No, no, no," Drake muttered, wringing out his hands. "This can't be happening."

"I don't think she appreciated being bitten," said Tattoos. "Looks like she brought along an assassin to help her kill you."

Drake's eyes shifted from Alex to Logan. Panic tore at his magic, sending out rocky waves of broken energy that bit at Alex's skin like a shower of pebbles. He shot a blast of crimson and silver Fairy Dust at the overhead lights, frying the system. The vampires playing with their guns grumbled in protest, but no one else seemed to care. Their kind was a nocturnal breed after all; they could see just fine in the dark.

The door at the other side of the room opened, flooding the area with UV-free daylight. As Drake rushed through the door, Alex sprinted forward, trying to catch him. She caught the door by her fingertips, throwing it open again. Her pulse pumping hard, she ran across the shooting field. Logan came up beside her, and together they tried to close the distance to Drake.

"And we have a champion, folks! Breena for the Fairy Division!" the loudspeakers roared.

The audience broke out in applause, and enthusiastic cheers poured down from the stadium seats. A bow-wielding fairy with bouncy golden hair looked up at her adoring fans and waved, her flower crown sliding sideways. A group of enamored human men in the front row whistled at her. She blew them a kiss, then turned, the skirt of her powder-pink lace and chiffon mini-dress bouncing against her thighs as she moved. Drake plowed right past her, angling for a door on the other side of the field.

He never made it.

Fire poured down from above, drenching him in flames. Horrid, tortured screams erupted from his mouth, the pain and terror of his dying cry turning Alex's stomach. Completely ablaze, the vampire elf ran a few steps before smacking against the wall with a decisive crunch.

Alex looked up. An enormous airborne dragon circled the stadium. He opened his mouth and flooded the field with fire.

CHAPTER TWELVE
Field of Fire

STREAMS OF FIRE rolled across the field, cascading like smashing rapids. Screaming fairies fled into the building. Two men lifted Breena, the fairy champion, onto their shoulders and carried her to safety beneath the audience's chorus.

"Save the fairy princess. Save the fairy princess," they chanted over the crackle of fire.

But as soon as Breena was inside, her spell shattered. Her adoring audience took their first clear-headed look at the dragon, then stampeded down the stairs in a raging panic.

"Ideas?" Logan asked Alex. "Monsters are your specialty."

They were the only two people left standing down there. The fire that had consumed most of the field hadn't reached them yet—but it was spreading fast.

Alex looked up. "That's not a real dragon."

"Of course not. There are no dragons anymore. It's dragon magic summoned by a mage."

"No," she said, reaching out her hand toward the

bonfire of flames. "It's not even that. It's an illusion."

"It sure looks real."

Ah, but sight was only a tiny piece of the magic pie. It was easiest one to fool, though. "Reach for the flames. They're not hot."

Logan extended his hand slowly, then quickly pulled it back. "They are hot."

"Really? Odd." Alex waved her hand through the flames. Magic prickled at her skin.

"Your hand is on fire."

"Is it?" she asked, looking down at her arm. Sure enough, flames licked up and down it. She shook it out, and the phantom fire dissolved.

"Does this have something to do with the super-secret magic you're pretending you don't have?"

Uh, probably. Oops. "No. I'm just more observant than you."

"Well, I observed that dragon setting the vampire elf on fire." Logan pointed at the charred corpse across the field. "He's dead."

"That was real fire."

"You're not making any sense."

"Maybe a mage piggybacked a spell on the illusion." She shrugged. "Don't you think it's awfully convenient that he happened to be set on fire right before we were going to talk to him? And then there were the thieves who attacked us. And the bartender at Impulse who was found dead before anyone could ask him anything about the Orbs."

"You think this is a conspiracy," he said.

"I sure as hell don't think it's a picnic. Someone is after the Orbs. And I think it's pretty obvious that someone will do whatever it takes—kill whoever it takes—to get what they want."

"There's someone up there." Logan nodded toward the now-empty audience seating.

Or maybe not so empty. "Is there?" She squinted into the stands. Sure enough, a cloaked figure lurked in a dark corner. "What do you want to bet that he's our illusionist?"

"Assassins don't bet," he replied coolly. "We act."

A gunshot echoed inside the dome. Alex scanned the area, honing in on a quartet of men standing at one of the four doors that fed into the field. They were all human, but they had really big guns.

From the way the humans were staring into the flames, they knew the fire wasn't real. But not because they could see through the illusion. Someone had told them. The fake heat was still bothering them. They were keeping to the edge of the field.

"Ok, you go *act* on those gunmen," she told Logan as she took off running toward stairs that led into the stands. "I'll take care of our hooded friend."

She sped up those stairs as fast as she could push herself. Seeing that running up stairs was a regular ingredient to her workouts, that was pretty damn fast. Her stubborn streak certainly didn't hurt either.

It wasn't enough.

She reached the right level, but the cloaked figure had already fled. Somehow. Alex didn't see any clear escape paths. Above, the dragon lingered on for a few seconds before its fiery form began to fade—then just winked out. A few more booms echoed off the glass walls, followed by a series of pained grunts. Logan sure hadn't wasted any time.

Metal scratched against the rough concrete floor, and Alex looked down to find a broken piece of silver beneath the toe of her boot. Other pieces—also broken—were scattered in an uneven circle, right where the cloaked figure had been standing. She slid on her leather gloves, then plucked one of the pieces from the ground. She held it lightly between two fingers, careful not to let the spiked edges puncture her gloves. Who knew what sort of magic was on them.

"Alex."

"Stop. Don't step on anything. I've found evidence here," she told Logan, turning the metal piece in front of her eyes. Magic always left a footprint. The question was whether her undeveloped powers could find it. "This is where the illusionist was standing." She pulled a felt bag off her belt and used her dagger to sweep the pieces into it. "We need to collect them and figure out what they mean."

"Alex," he said again, his voice uneven.

She spun around just in time to catch him as he fell. Blood drenched the front of his left pant leg, where a bullet had torn through his thigh.

CHAPTER THIRTEEN
Pixie Magic

EVERYONE HAD FLED the Glass Dome—including the medical personnel—so there was no one to take care of Logan's wounds. Alex patched him up as best she could, dumped him into the passenger seat of his Maserati, then screeched out of the parking lot like an enraged hell beast.

"You're driving my car," Logan muttered, his eyelids sliding down.

Alex grabbed the ice scraper from the door pocket; it was black. She rolled her eyes. Assassins. She reached over and poked him in the shoulder with the dull end.

"Damn it, woman!" he shouted, jumping in his seat. At least his eyes were open again. "Are you insane? You don't just go around poking assassins."

She shrugged. "If you don't want to get poked, then stay awake. I know someone who can fix you up, but you need to hold it together until we get there."

"I hope you don't mean that dragon summoner you work with. I've seen what happens when he tries to heal people." Logan paled—or maybe it was the blood loss.

"No, not Marek. He's not even here right now. I'm

bringing you to Daisy."

"You'll have to be more specific."

"Daisy Goldcast."

This time, he definitely paled. "That might not be the best idea."

"Please tell me you didn't kill anyone she cares about."

"I didn't."

"Or otherwise assault, torture, or maim them."

"No."

Alex spun the car into a sharp u-turn, sliding across the tram tracks to speed down the other side of the road.

"Slow down. There's a speed camera up ahead," he warned her.

"You've been shot, and you're worried about a speeding ticket?"

"Yes. If this wound doesn't do me in, the speeding fine just might. They charge a percentage of your income."

"That bites." Alex slowed down, sticking her tongue out at the speed camera as they passed. "I hear a grumpy old ghost is running the transportation department nowadays."

"I doubt the city government would hire a supernatural."

"The guy ran the department when he was alive. Then one day, he woke up dead. They tried to fire him—you know, on account of his being dead and all. But he wouldn't have it. He haunted the city government meetings until they caved in."

"You have a unique imagination, Alex."

"Who me? Nah, I'm blunt as a stone." She poked him once more because his head was starting to drop again.

"You're testing my patience," he growled. "Poke me with that thing once more, and I'll snap it in half."

"Temper, temper. There's no need to assassinate the

poor ice scraper," she said, sliding into the only available parking spot in front of Daisy's building. Thank goodness for Sundays. There was never any parking during the week.

Alex opened the car door, stepping out into the city's Industrial District. The name was something of a misnomer, a fallback to an earlier era. Most of the industrial work had been ejected from the city years ago—and the pixies, the workers of metal and magic, went with it. The industrial-style buildings, however, had remained.

She mashed the button beside the front entrance a few times. A few seconds later, the door creaked open, and a black-haired pixie in a powder-blue cardigan stepped outside. She was short; the top of her tight bun only reached Alex's bellybutton.

Like all fairies, pixies had the look of youth about them. Her face was that of a teenager, but her eyes said she'd been around a lot longer. Decades? Centuries? Her magic tasted like metal and hummed like a well-tuned engine.

"No need to rush, dear," Daisy said, her voice as old as her eyes.

"I have a bleeding assassin in the car," Alex told her.

The pixie blinked once. "And now you want me to hide the body? Alex, you really must be more careful with that sword of yours."

"He's not dead. He's been shot, and I need you to heal him."

Daisy looked into the car. "That's not just any assassin you've got there, dear. That's Slayer."

Logan stared back at her, his eyes cool. The perfect assassin.

"Can you heal him?" Alex asked.

"I'll try. But first we need to move this car. Bloody Bob

will burst a vein if he sees you parked in his spot."

"Bloody Bob?"

"The vampire next door." Daisy flicked her hand at the garage door. The vines covering it slithered back, and the door rolled up. "Bob's a stickler for rules—most especially the ones he made up himself. And he's decided that this spot is his." With her other hand, she waved the car toward the open door. It obeyed her commands, sliding smoothly into the garage. Pixies had a way with all things made of metal.

"Your neighbor sounds like a real treat," Alex told her.

Tiny Daisy lifted Logan out of the car, as though his solid body of muscle weighed no more than a rag doll. She set him on the sofa in her garage. Yes, she had a sofa in her garage. She had all kinds of other furniture here too. Like a kitchen bar with a bowl full of fruit on top. And a flat panel television.

"You should see how livid he gets when I vacuum on a Sunday," Daisy said, looking down at Logan's leg.

"His building isn't touching yours. How can he even hear the vacuum cleaner?"

"Damn vampires and their super senses." Daisy began to unravel Logan's bandages. "Alex, dear, generally one puts the bandage *under* the patient's clothing, not over."

"I'm not a doctor. I hack things apart with my sword," she replied. "Besides, I didn't have time for that. He was bleeding too much, and there was no one there to heal him. They all ran away when that hooded guy unleashed a dragon on the Glass Dome."

"A dragon?"

"An illusion of a dragon. He used some sort of…magic artifact? I'll show it to you later."

"Goody." The bloody bandages removed, Daisy pulled

out a pair of scissors and began to cut the fabric away from Logan's wound. "There's no exit hole. The bone's been hit." She looked at Logan. "How are you still conscious?"

"A crazy mercenary kept poking me with an ice scraper."

Daisy snorted. "Good for her." She set her hand over the wound. "I can heal you. There will be a price, though."

"How much do you want?"

"Not that kind of price. I owe Alex on account of the zombies, so I'll fix you up for free. I mean, to heal something as bad as this, I'll need to draw on some of your energy. After I'm done, you might doze off."

"I understand."

A silvery glow spread across Daisy's hands, pouring into the bloody hole in Logan's thigh. The blood around the wound dried up, then dissolved.

"What were you doing at Supernatural Steel?" the pixie asked.

"Investigating," said Alex.

"Investigating, huh?" She plucked out the bullet that had risen to the wound's surface. Glowing stitches of crisscrossing magic spread across the hole, merging the skin together.

"Does that usually involve getting shot at?"

"My whole lifestyle involves getting shot at," Alex replied. "And sword fighting. And dodging destructive magic. And monsters spitting weird goo at me."

"Have you ever considered switching careers?"

"Besides killing monsters, I don't have any marketable skills. I doubt they'd appreciate my knack for killing misbehaving supernaturals at places like Wizard House Pizza or Madam Meringue's. Hell, most of their customers probably are misbehaving supernaturals."

"Probably," agreed Daisy. "Ok, I'm done." She lifted her hands, shaking the last remaining glowing glitter from her fingertips.

Alex looked Logan's leg. "Amazing. You can't even tell he was shot."

"Do you want me to take a look at your arm?" Daisy pointed at the hole in Alex's jacket.

"Sure," she said, slipping out of her jacket.

Daisy took a long, hard look at the cuts on her arm. "Were you attacked by a swarm of glass hornets?"

"No. I was standing too close to a mage when he blew up a glass candle cover."

"This happened today?"

"Yes. Before the tournament."

"Alex, how many fights have you been in today?"

"Well…"

"You don't remember?"

"Not really."

"Three," Logan said.

"One of those fights was with you, you crazy assassin."

"You initiated the fight."

"No, you initiated it by locking me up in chains."

His sigh was ripe with exasperation. "We've been over this already. I did that so you couldn't attack me as soon as you woke up."

"Ha! Well, the joke was on you, wasn't it? Because I did just that!"

"Not immediately. We had a fine chat before that."

Daisy tapped her finger to Alex's arm. A wave of comforting warmth filled her, its embrace like a nice, fuzzy blanket.

"That should do it," the pixie said. "The magic is still repairing your cells. Do try to stay out of trouble for the rest of the day. No more fights, at least until tomorrow."

Alex planted her hands on her hips. "Hey, it's not like I asked all those people to attack me."

"Just yesterday, you flung rocks at a gang of vampire elves," Logan said.

"So? They'd looted a fairy building and were getting away. I had to get their attention somehow."

"That was asking them to attack you."

"You need to put the brakes on that recklessness of yours," Daisy said.

Logan winked at Alex.

"Aren't you supposed to be sleeping?" she told him.

"I feel just fine."

Daisy looked into his eyes. "No exhaustion?" She felt his forehead. "Dizziness?"

"No."

"Remarkable. I've never seen a human take to healing magic this well. There's always some rejection. But not with you. Your body just sucked it up like a sponge. This didn't happen last time."

"Last time?" Alex asked.

He cupped his hands behind his head and leaned back into the armrest. "I'm hungry."

"Of course you are. And I have just the thing." Daisy walked off toward the kitchen bar, returning with a plate full of brownies. "I just made these this morning."

Logan began to eat the brownies. He didn't shovel them into his mouth, but he was efficient. Only an assassin could eat something that fast without looking like he was rushing it. Alex watched him with strange fascination.

"You said you had something for me to look at," Daisy reminded her.

"Right." She removed the pouch of metal shards from

her belt. "We found these right where the illusionist who summoned the dragon was standing."

Daisy spilled out the contents of the bag onto the coffee table beside the sofa. She waved her hand, and the pieces floated up, bobbing up and down like debris on the ocean's surface.

"What are they?" Alex asked her, reaching for a brownie on Logan's plate.

He caught her by the wrist before she could touch it. "Mine."

"You could share just one."

"Fine." He released her hand.

Alex snatched the brownie before he had a chance to change his mind. "Daisy?"

The pixie leaned in to get a closer look at the floating pieces. "It's enchanted metal."

"Someone spelled it?"

"No. Mages can spell objects, but the magic only lasts for a short time before it evaporates from the metal. Pixies enchant things, forging magic into the metal itself. The effect is permanent."

"Could an object be enchanted to create the illusion of a dragon?"

"It depends on how big the illusion is and how complete."

"Big," Alex said.

She took a bite of the brownie, and magic exploded in her mouth. There was enough kick in that one bite to send a first tier mage sky-high on magic. She set it back down on the plate, and Logan tossed it into his mouth.

"How can you eat that?" she asked him.

"Delicious." He grabbed another.

She shook her head in disbelief. "You're like a black

hole for magic."

"Intriguing," Daisy said, watching him eat the brownies. "No one's ever finished more than one." She turned her scientific eye on Alex. "You're acting strangely normal."

"I'm a magic dud."

"Hmm." She picked up the nearest brownie and gave it a sniff. "Smells normal. Tell me more about your dragon illusion, Alex."

"Right. So it was big. And it was a pretty complex illusion, covering all five senses. It had everyone fooled."

"Except Alex," Logan said between bites. "The fire didn't just look real. It felt hot too. And I could smell things burning."

"Sounds like a really good illusion." Daisy waved her hand above the metal pieces, and they began to spin. A soft, silver hum buzzed from them. "Yes, the enchantment in this metal is strong. First tier alone wouldn't cut it to see through an illusion like that. Only the most powerful first tier mages—I'd guess a fraction of a percent—could do it."

Alex could feel Logan watching her. She silenced the panicking voices in her head and tried to keep her mind on the metal pieces.

"Could you put the pieces together to make the object it once was?" she asked Daisy.

"Of course I can." She swirled her finger around, and the pieces spun faster. There was a flash of light, then a metal ball the size of an orange was floating where the pieces had just been. "Here it is."

"What is it?" Alex asked her.

"I don't recognize this object."

That was saying a lot. Daisy was the city's expert on magical objects. It took something really bizarre to stump her.

"Oh, no."

Alex turned to look at Logan. He was staring at the object. His face was even more unreadable than usual, which meant whatever emotions he was trying to hide must have been pretty strong.

"You recognize this?" she asked him.

"The object, no. But the symbol…" He brushed his finger across the subtle engraving on the side of the ball. "That is the symbol of the Convictionites. They're the ones behind this. They're the ones who are after the Orbs."

"Convictionites?"

"They're like…well, a cult, I suppose you could call it. Though they like to refer to themselves as a secret society. Or a kingdom. The organization is made up exclusively of humans. It's an old cult. They've known about the existence of supernaturals for centuries, long before the rest of the world found out."

"I take it they aren't friendly to the idea of living in a world with magic?" Alex asked.

"No, they distrust it. And since they knew about magic long before the rest of the human population, they've had some time to find ways to fight it."

"Why do they want the orbs?"

"I don't know."

"Gaelyn says the Orbs are made with powerful magic," Alex said. "So why would the Convictionites want them? That doesn't sound like the behavior of people who hate magic."

"Their logo is printed on this magical object," Daisy pointed out.

"I can't explain that," said Logan.

"It's been too long of a day for me to try to explain

anything." Alex stood up from the sofa, stretching out her arms. "It's getting late. I'm going home now. Thanks, Daisy." She snatched up the object and slid it into the largest of her pouches. "I'll chat with Gaelyn about this, then we can start again tomorrow."

"You're going to have to drive him home," Daisy called out to her.

Alex turned around. "He looks fine."

"I healed him, yes, but his body has undergone a severe trauma. That bullet took a chip out of his femur. Not only am I surprised he didn't pass out, I'm shocked he wasn't screaming in agony."

"He's an assassin. They're all a bit mental."

"I'll take that as a compliment," Logan said, grabbing another brownie.

Alex wasn't even sure which of them he was responding to.

"I think that's enough for you." Daisy snatched the brownie out of his hand. She ignored the cold look he gave her. "Even if he hadn't just been shot, he's eaten far too many of those to drive."

"Fine." Alex opened the car door. "Let's go, Logan."

CHAPTER FOURTEEN
Assassin's Place

"I THINK THE brownies are wearing off," Logan said. "My leg is waking up."

Alex turned the car into his driveway. "Just in time. Where's the remote for this garage door?"

"Next to the Witch Slayers."

She nudged the bundle of throwing knives aside and fished the remote out of the cup holder. "Do you typically keep a lot of weapons in your car?"

"Sure. Just not as many as I keep on me."

The garage door slid open, and Alex drove down into the underground garage. It had enough parking spots for twenty cars. Even though half of them were empty, she didn't need to ask which one was his. The enormous sign stapled to the fence of the neighboring storage cage left no doubt. It read, 'I generally won't kill someone for under seven figures, but if you touch my things, I'll do the job for free. You have been warned.'

It was signed with a big, cursive S. In red. Alex shook her head. Crazy assassin.

"What's in there?" she asked Logan, pointing at the

cage.

"Some spare furniture."

"All that…" She waved at the sign. "…for a few pieces of furniture?"

"It's not about the furniture. It's about the image. The day people think they can mess with my things will be the end of my career. No one wants to hire an assassin people aren't afraid of."

"You have a good relationship with your neighbors, do you?"

He shrugged. "They don't bother me."

In other words, they were all scared shitless of him.

"On the other hand," he said. "No one would dare attack this building. Even the monsters know to stay away."

"Just one of the perks of living in the same building as a notorious assassin?"

"Are you always this sarcastic?"

"Of course."

He didn't smile, but she could tell he really wanted to. "Well, it is one of your more endearing qualities."

"Along with slashing monsters."

"I do love a woman who can decapitate an enormous sea slug."

"It was a sea serpent."

He reached over and patted her arm. "Sure it was, sweetheart."

As his hand slid down to her fingertips, her pulse prickled against her skin. This time, he did smile—and it was a knowing sort of smile. Her heart was pounding hard and heavy, her head spinning with crazy thoughts.

She swung open the door and jumped out of the car. Being so close to him was…unnerving. Yeah, that was the word. Not thrilling. And most definitely not tempting.

Assassins weren't tempting. They were scary. Scary and crazy.

"So, I'll see you tomorrow," she said awkwardly, not looking back at him as she headed for the door.

"Alex."

He was right beside her. Too close. Again. She could feel the heat evaporating off his body.

"I have to go."

"Wait," he said, grabbing her wrist.

She spun around, trying not to see him.

"How am I going to make it up all those stairs in my *condition*?" he asked, drawing out the last word. His face was perfectly serious, but there was just something about his aura… Amusement?

"You seem fine. And there's an elevator." She tried to pry his hand off her wrist—and failed. He had an iron grip. "Let go."

"Why?"

He was playing games with her. And playing with an assassin was a really bad idea.

"Either you let go, or I will draw my sword and make you let go," she said.

He laughed, releasing her arm. "We're not as different as you tell yourself we are."

"Goodnight, Logan."

"You need to see me safely home. *All* the way home. Doctor's orders."

"I don't think Daisy meant I had to tuck you into your bed for the night."

He pulled out his phone. "Shall we ask her?"

"No." Daisy would probably say she had, in fact, meant just that. Pixies got a kick out of playing silly tricks like that.

Alex headed for the elevator and pressed the button. The sooner this was over with, the better.

"Which floor?" she asked as they walked inside the elevator.

"Top."

Penthouse suite. Of course. She hit the top button. The smooth hum of the climbing elevator filled the empty silence. Alex tried to stand still—and not to fidget. Across the very tiny cabin, the assassin was watching her like she was his next target.

"So," she said quickly. "How do you know Daisy?"

The gleam in his eyes didn't die down, even as he responded, "Daisy and I go way back. I met her years ago, back when I first arrived in Zurich. I came here to take on my first job as an assassin."

"How did it go?"

"Not well. I really didn't know anything back then. I got pretty badly torn up."

"More than today?"

"Yes, a lot more than today. Daisy fixed me up. She told me how stupid I'd been. She said I was physically strong, but I acted dumb. I didn't like her very much for that, but it was what I needed to hear. In my line of work, an overinflated ego is essentially a death sentence."

She snorted. "You realize your ego is bigger than anyone's, right?"

"That's not ego. It's fact. I know precisely what I can and cannot do. I just happen to be able to do a lot more than basically anyone."

"Right. Just give me a chance to fight you after I haven't been tied up in chains all night, and we'll see who comes up on top."

"I'd love to have you come up on top, darling."

The look in his eyes almost made her turn away, but she was too stubborn to lose a staring contest with an assassin. Especially that assassin.

"I'll bring my sword," she said, tapping her fingers across her arms.

"I'll bring my knives." A smile slid across his lips. "Or would you prefer to grapple without our weapons."

And without our clothes. She could almost hear the unsaid suggestion lingering on his lips. She wished he would just say it outright, so she could punch him in the face. But an assassin never attacked directly. He slid past your defenses, his movements unseen until it was too late.

The elevator doors opened, and she hopped out. She took only two steps before the hallway ended in a door. Logan's hand brushed past her hip, and she jumped.

"Relax, hun. I'm just opening the door." He slid his key into the lock.

"What happened next with Daisy?" she asked, forcing her spiraling thoughts back on track.

He swung the door open, then waved her inside. "After she fixed me up, she told me where I needed to go to learn how to not get myself killed."

"Where?"

"Have you heard of the Veiled?"

"It's an order of assassins."

"It's *the* order of assassins." He trailed her into the apartment and flipped on the lights. "The best assassins in the world. I trained under them for several years, then returned to Europe to work as an independent assassin."

"Where are they?"

"Far away," he said vaguely. "I'm sworn to secrecy. I cannot reveal the location of their base." He walked toward the kitchen. "Would you like something to drink?"

Alex stared out of his living room window. They were high above the city. Below, white and yellow lights stretched out like a twinkling carpet, hugging the shores of the lake. As dark as black ice, the water looked almost peaceful—if only she hadn't known about the monsters lurking beneath the surface.

Logan's living room was no less spectacular than the view. A border of leafy gold and red details surrounded the edges of the glossy marble floors. The furniture was a classy mix of leather and wood, and there were enough gadgets to fill an electronics store.

"Alex?"

She turned around to find him standing there with a glass of pale pink liquid in his hand.

"Thirsty?" he asked.

"What is it?"

He handed her the glass. "Water with strawberry and peppermint."

"Is that all?" She sniffed the drink. It smelled sweet and minty.

"No, I'm trying to drug you." He rolled his eyes. "Of course that's all. You have real trust issues, don't you?"

"Oh, forgive my caution," she growled. "I woke up this morning after being drugged and chained down in an old warehouse."

"I didn't drug you. It was the bartender from Impulse."

"Who's dead now, so I can't even confirm that he did it."

"Are you questioning my honor?"

"Are you questioning my intelligence?" she shot back. "Because forgive me if I don't take the word of an assassin when he claims he didn't kill someone."

"Have I given you any reason not to trust me?"

106

"You chained me up."

He sighed. "Besides that."

"Besides that? Do you ever listen to yourself talk? You chained me up all night in a freaking factory, you psychopath."

"You passed out. I got you out of Impulse before Hugh or anyone else tried to kill you."

"And the chains?"

"You sure are crotchety, aren't you? Just so you know, you didn't spend the night in chains. You slept on a sofa. And when you started to wake up, I put you in the chains so you wouldn't attack me."

"You could have just brought me home."

"And have you believe I tried to poison you?" he said. "I wanted to work with you, which could only happen if you agreed to speak with me."

"So you decided to force a conversation by tying me up?"

He frowned. "Well, when you put it like that, of course it sounds bad."

"There is no other way to put it!"

"Will it help if I apologize?"

"That depends on what you say."

"Alexandria Dering, please allow me to express my deepest remorse for restraining you for my own selfish purposes. I hereby swear to never tie you up again—" He grinned. "—without your permission."

"Very pretty apology," she told him.

"Do you accept it?"

"Fine. Whatever."

She took a sip of her drink. The taste of peppermint chased strawberry across her tongue. It was good. She took another sip, looking around the apartment.

"Being an assassin sure must pay well," she commented.

He slipped off his jacket, tossing it onto the sofa. "It does."

Alex kept her eyes up—and far, far away from his body. Corded muscle, taut and hard, stretched across his body, pressing against his shirt. Every line, every curve and dip, was etched into the skintight fabric.

"I could use a partner," he said. "Interested?"

Yes, please. Wait, no. Alex shook her head. So much for not looking at him.

As she met his smile, she decided two things. Firstly, there was something indecent in that smile. And secondly —more troubling—that she liked it. She set her glass down and started to back away before she could do something really stupid. Like even more stupid than going home with an assassin.

"Are you sure you don't want to stay?" he asked, following her.

"I'm sure."

Then she opened the door and ran out.

CHAPTER FIFTEEN
Reckless

ALEX HURRIED HOME and went straight to bed. But she couldn't escape the assassin. He followed her into her dreams.

She stood barefoot on Logan's roof terrace, looking down at the twinkling city lights as she sipped strawberry-peppermint water. She was dressed in a tennis skirt and a thin tank top. For some strange reason, she wasn't wearing underwear. Or a bra.

A cool breeze slid across her skin, shooting icicles to every tip of her body. She shivered.

"Cold?"

Strong, warm arms embraced her from behind. She leaned back into the assassin, resting her head on his bare chest.

"No," she said.

A chuckle rumbled deep in his chest. "Alex." He turned her around to face him. "You're being reckless again."

"By spending time with you?"

"Yes." His hand caressed her jaw, following the line down her neck. "Assassins are dangerous." His fingers massaged the back of her head, slowly working her hair free of the ponytail.

"Mmm."

"We're a bad influence." He kissed her softly, his lips teasing hers before pulling away.

She arched forward, following him. "I know."

"Alex." He inhaled deeply. "You aren't wearing any underwear."

"How do you know?"

"Enhanced senses, remember?" He took another deep breath. "You should know better than to taunt an assassin."

Alex's breath hiccuped as his hands slid down her butt.

"We always rise to the challenge." He slipped one hand between her legs and drew a burning line down the inside of her thigh.

"Logan," she moaned, willing him to move his hand back up.

"We don't shy away, don't hesitate."

"But you do tease."

His green eyes flashed. "Yes. Oh, Alex, you can't even imagine how much I want you."

The barrier holding back her magic crackled as it began to fracture. "Sure…I can."

"You want me too," he said smugly.

Molten magic bubbled beneath her skin like magma.

"Say it."

"I want you," she admitted. Her magic thumped and burned, trying to break past the crumbling barrier. "Now are you going to kiss me or what?"

"Oh, I'm going to do so much more than kiss you, darling." His lips brushed against her neck. "You thought this was teasing? Seduction is a six-course meal, and this was only the appetizer."

Alex's pulse spiked as he kissed the inside of her wrist. Her blood was burning in her veins.

"I have all night," he said with a leisurely smile. "And I'm going to string you up so tight that a single touch will make you explode."

She leaned in and bit him on the lip. A crimson drop dangled from his mouth, daring her to lick it. She didn't even try to resist it.

"Alex," he growled.

She could feel the desire pouring off of him like magic. She bit him again. Roaring, he slammed her against the window. His hands tore at her clothes, impatient and unchecked.

"How long have you been thinking about me?" he asked, tossing her shirt off the balcony.

She pressed herself against him. Magic poured down her arms, supercharging every nerve in her body.

He leaned back, evading her lips. "How long?"

"Logan," she protested and dropped her head.

He balanced a finger beneath her chin and pushed up until she met his eyes. "Alex, how long?"

"Since we fought that pack of werewolves."

A satisfied smile cut across his lips. "So the first day we met."

"Yes."

"Good. The first step is admitting it to yourself."

"The first step? The first step to wh—"

His kiss swallowed her words; his touch overrode her mind. And as his hands slid beneath her skirt, her magic exploded. Light and color clashed and erupted in a dizzying array of fireworks that popped her ears and scorched her blood.

She stumbled and fell. The dream shattered.

Her shoulder hit the ground, sliding against smooth wood. She tried to stand up but tripped over the blanket twisted around her legs. She reached up to the light switch and clicked the table lamp on. Kicking off the blanket, she stood, then walked across the bedroom to the wall mirror.

"Idiot," she said, looking into the mirror.

Her breath was heavy and strained. The aftershock of her magic still sizzled on her skin.

"Idiot," she said again, touching her reflection in the mirror. "What's the matter with you?"

She shouldn't be having dreams about Logan—especially not *those* sort of dreams. She smacked her hands against her legs, trying to shake out the last lingering remains of magic. Fantasizing about him apparently made her magic go haywire.

Stupid, stupid, stupid, she chastised herself, slapping her cheeks a few times.

She was supposed to be hiding her magic. Getting high on magic while making out with Logan—even if only in her dreams—was not hiding it.

"You're pathetic," she told her reflection as she put on a new top. One that didn't smell like him.

She hadn't even changed out of her battle-worn clothes when she'd gotten home after fleeing—no, making a strategic retreat from Logan's place. Fleeing was for cowards. Which she was not.

You are so, said a voice in her head.

"Shut up."

If she'd stayed with him any longer, things would have gotten complicated. Her dream proved that. She didn't trust that assassin—and she trusted herself when she was with him even less.

Marek was right. Killing monsters twenty-four seven

was not a life. She needed to get out more. She needed to go out on a date once in a while—or, at the very least, have meaningless sex once in a while.

Like with the assassin? the voice suggested.

Alex shook her head. Bad idea. Very bad idea. Like apocalypse bad. She couldn't let herself get close to him. There was no way he could be trusted. He chased big ticket bounties, and the bounty on a Dragon Born mage was the highest the Magic Council offered.

Who said anything about trust? This is about meaningless sex, remember? And you want the assassin.

"No."

The voice snickered in her head. *There's no point in lying. The two of you are so hot for each other, it's distracting even me. I don't enjoy being flooded with your hormones. How many times are you going to fantasize about running your hands down his ripped abs before you do it? Just jump his bones and be done with it. Then you'll be able to concentrate on keeping us alive.*

"Us? Who are you?" she asked the voice.

Never mind that. Just know that I'm right.

"Sera?" The voice sounded a lot like her sister.

No.

"Does this have anything to do with me being Dragon Born?"

This has to do with you being crazy. Only crazy people talk to themselves.

Since she couldn't frown at the mystery voice, she frowned at her own reflection instead. She figured the voice would see it.

Of course I see it. And it's very rude to frown at people who are trying to help you.

"Suggesting that I have sex with a murderous assassin is

not helping."

If voices could shrug, this one would have. *That's redundant.*

"What is?"

Murderous assassin. Assassins are killers by definition. That's like saying cold ice.

"I'm not going to argue semantics with the voice in my head."

Agreed. Stop arguing and just do as I say. It's seven o'clock in the evening.

"And?" Alex was so beat that she'd fallen asleep as soon as she'd gotten home. Fighting for your life was an exhausting hobby.

You were only asleep for a few minutes. Your dirty mind went right to that assassin.

"How is insulting me helping at all?"

Mages have turned lucid dreaming into an art. Go to sleep and force that dream to pick up right where it left off.

"No." Alex shook her head—perhaps a bit too vigorously. Her neck cracked. "I'm not going to have dream sex with Logan."

Why not? Dream Logan isn't a threat to you. You can just pull him out when you need him, pump out your frustration, then put him away again when you're done. No risk of death, betrayal, or rug burns.

"You're demented."

I'm a voice in your head, dear. I'm only as demented as you make me.

Damn.

What do you say? The night is young. You can probably bang him at least a dozen times before sunrise.

Alex rushed toward the bathroom. She didn't need to fantasize about sleeping with Logan. What she needed was a shower. And maybe a snack. Like chocolate.

Good idea. Chocolate is a fantastic aphrodisiac.

Scrap the chocolate. She'd make herself a hamburger. With lots of ketchup.

Mmm, ketchup. The assassin can lick it off your lips like you did to his blood.

"I liked you better when I thought you were just a figment of my imagination."

Who says I'm not? Maybe I'm your fun side.

Before Alex could argue further with the voice, a wailing siren cut through the night. The security alarm from Gaelyn's house. She spun around and ran for the window.

Light flashed through the curtain. She threw it back and looked outside. All the floodlights were on in the garden that separated the guest house, where she was staying, from the main house. Light poured out of every window in Gaelyn's house too.

Alex stumbled into her boots on her way to the door. Grabbing her sword, she sprinted down the path toward Gaelyn's house—and toward the flames licking the frame of the broken living room window.

CHAPTER SIXTEEN
Turned

ALEX SLUNK THROUGH the living room, wading through a curtain of steam. There was smoke everywhere but not much fire. Gaelyn stood beside the burning window, spraying the last remaining flames with the fire extinguisher.

"What happened?" she asked him.

"Explosion." A wheezy cough cracked his lips.

Alex opened a window, then moved on to the next. "An attack?" She hadn't seen any evidence that Gaelyn's defenses had been breached. In fact, besides the ominous smoke lingering in the air, the living room looked pretty much untouched.

"No. It came from the basement. I looked through the security footage." The look on his face was foreboding.

"And?" she asked. "What was it?"

"The enchanted object you brought back. It exploded."

"I..." She choked on the guilt. "I'm sorry, Gaelyn. I thought you could figure out more about it. I knew it was dangerous, but I didn't think it would explode. I was stupid."

He set his hand on her shoulder. "Alexandria, it's not your fault. We play a dangerous game. There are risks. We all know that. Thankfully, no one was hurt. Everything else can be repaired."

"I should have warned you."

"No, this happened because of me. I've grown so weak. I can't even sense objects properly anymore. The millennia have whittled away at my magic. It's fading, slowly but surely. Soon, it will be completely gone." He sounded resigned—and tired. Really tired.

Sirens wailed outside. Alex looked through the broken window as a fire truck rolled up to the gate. "The fire department is here."

"Holt will let them in." Gaelyn plopped onto one of the stools at the bar, his legs collapsing like he hadn't slept in days. "You're hungry."

"How did you know?"

"Now that your adrenaline has crashed, your stomach is growling." He waved toward the kitchen. "Help yourself."

"Thanks." She headed for the refrigerator. "Do you want anything?"

"A bottle of wine."

She glanced back at him. "How close were you to the explosion?"

"Too close." He reached up to the rack hanging over the bar and plucked a wine glass from it. "I'm getting too old for all this excitement."

Alex grabbed a big yogurt container, a spoon, and a bottle of Gaelyn's favorite wine. As she sat down beside him, Holt waved an entourage of firemen into the house to look over the damage. But he lingered in the doorway.

"Is he still squeamish about fire?" Alex asked Gaelyn.

"A pair of elemental mages set him on fire. I don't

believe he will get over that so easily."

Probably not. Holt was a vampire. The only thing vampires hated more than fire, was being set on fire. They weren't too fond of mages who set them on fire either.

"What's going on with the Orbs of Essence?" She popped the lid off the yogurt container. "What are the Mage Triad and the Circle of the Otherworldly doing to protect the remaining two?"

"They assure me they have implemented additional security measures."

"What kind of security measures?" She scooped up a spoonful of pink yogurt and ate it. Mmm, strawberry.

"Up until now, they've all been using magic security systems from Drachenburg Industries. However, given the recent break-ins at that company, the mages and the otherworldly have switched to a White Knight solution."

"Never heard of them."

"They're a small private company." He poured himself a glass of wine. "They specialize in security that implements a mix of tech and magic defenses."

"Will it be enough?"

He shook his head. "Alexandria, I really can't say. Maybe. It depends on what we're up against."

Alex pointed at the broken and burnt living room. "That's what we're up against. A hate group." When she'd gotten home earlier, she'd been too tired to tell him everything she and Logan had learned. "They're called the Convictionites. The logo of their organization was engraved into the enchanted ball that blew up your basement."

"The Convictionites." He sucked in a deep breath, his pale face growing paper thin. "Their organization preaches that magic is evil."

"And yet they are after magical objects. What do they

want with them?" she asked. "To use them to kill the city's supernaturals?"

"They hate magic, Alexandria. People who hate magic don't use it. They destroy it."

"What would happen if they destroyed the Orbs?"

He took a long drink from his glass. "No one can say for sure. The Orbs of Essence were created to maintain the balance of magic in the world. Without them, the balance might dissolve. If that happens, instinct would override reason; chaos would tear down order."

"If they're so dangerous, why didn't the Magic Council better protect the Orbs?" she demanded. "Why do they keep them in bars and old factory buildings?"

"The Orbs are so old that they've almost been elevated to myth status. The Council sees them as a symbol, nothing else." He sipped from his wine glass. "And maybe they're right. Maybe the Orbs are as I am: so old that they no longer hold any true power."

"And if the Council is wrong? If the Orbs still maintain the balance?"

"Then their destruction would be the end of our world as we know it today."

"You said instinct would override reason. Supernaturals would go mad?"

"Perhaps. It depends on the supernatural—and their instincts. Some of them are more violent than others."

"Like the vampires," she said.

"Yes."

"The Convictionites already have the Blood Orb. If they destroy it, will the vampires go into collective bloodlust?"

"If the Orbs still hold power, that's very likely," he said calmly, swirling the wine in his glass.

"Damn it, Gaelyn." She pounded her fist so hard against the bar that her spoon buzzed against the marble countertop. "We're talking about a complete breakdown of the magical order. We could be looking at a worldwide bloodbath. How can you be so calm?"

"Three reasons," he said. "Firstly, panicking doesn't help. We're doing everything we can to prevent this from happening. Secondly, we don't know if the Orbs still hold that kind of power. And finally—most importantly—it's basically impossible to destroy them. They're impervious to mundane weapons and resistant to magic."

"How resistant?"

"Extremely. A horde of first tier mages could shoot destructive magic at the Orbs all day, and they wouldn't even make a dent in them. The same goes for the fairies, vampires, and otherworldly. No one has that much magic anymore."

"Do you?"

"No. Not anymore. Long ago, yes, perhaps I could have done it. But no longer." His eyes drifted upward, as if he were remembering better days. He shook his head, breaking free of the nostalgia. "There have been many powerful supernaturals over the ages. The dragons. They probably could have done it. But they're gone too. No one has seen a real dragon in centuries."

"What happened to them?"

He had to know. He'd been around longer than anyone. He'd witnessed the rise and fall of empires—magical and mundane.

"It is a sad tale, Alexandria." He stared into his empty glass. "Let's not speak of it."

She wanted to ask him about the Dragon Born, but she had a feeling his answer would be the same. Besides, she knew what had happened to her kind. The evil overlords of the Magic Council had killed every last one of them. The Convictionites weren't the only ones who hated what they didn't understand.

"Whatever Convictionites can or cannot do to the Orbs, the fact remains that we can't let them have the others. And we need to take back the ones they've stolen," she said.

"The Convictionites are a danger," he agreed, pouring himself another glass of wine. "They could disrupt the entire supernatural order. I've heard things. Whispers of terrible things."

"What terrible things?"

"They capture and torture supernaturals. But the cries do not travel far. They are quickly silenced."

"What do they want?"

"To rip magic from the face of the earth," he said. "I don't know how they plan to do it. Perhaps they think the Orbs will help with that. All I know is the seed of hatred they planted in Europe is spreading. The poison of their cause is spreading."

"What can we do to stop them?"

He gave her a tired smile. "You are already doing it. You are fighting the monsters of the magical world, the vile beasts that attack the humans without reason or restraint, turning them against us. It's a long battle. A hard battle. And Zurich has been hit especially hard. You've seen it?"

"There are more monsters here than back home," she agreed. "And more supernaturals who should know better than to misbehave."

"It's already changed the humans' attitudes toward us," he said. "In most of the world, they aspire to be us. Here, many of them fear us. And that fear is spreading. Deep down, all humans fear what they do not understand. Us. So far, the fear has been covered up by their desire to be like us. Hope is a powerful thing, but the charade is already wearing thin, no small thanks to people like the Convictionites. Soon the awe and wonder humanity feels for the supernatural will wither and die, and only the fear will remain."

"You think the battle has already been lost," she realized.

He sighed. "It is not a single battle. It is a war against human nature. And it will not be won easily."

"We can't give up," she insisted. "If we lose—if the haters win—then the real war will begin. And millions will die."

"We'll do what we can." He patted her arm. "Alexandria, I need your help. You are making a difference here."

She let out a pained laugh. "It doesn't seem that way. Every day, there are more monsters. And they are getting tougher. Like the hybrids."

"I will hire more people to handle the monsters, but there just aren't any other mercenaries like you. You've been here for two months. None of your predecessors lasted more than two weeks."

She swallowed hard. "Killed in action?"

"Some of them. The others quit. I picked the best of the best, mages and fairies and vampires who had the highest combat magic ratings in the world. And do you know what I found out?"

"That combat magic ratings are complete bullshit?"

He chuckled. "Precisely. I should have known better than to blindly trust the system. I helped set up that system, and I knew there were flaws. There are always flaws.

These mercenaries had flashy magic and impressive resumes, but not one of them has your willpower."

"Some call it stubbornness," she said.

"Stubbornness. Willpower. Endurance. The fact remains that most powerful mages burn hot, then flicker out. They don't have what it takes to keep going, even when the end is nowhere in sight. Not one of them knows what it's like to fight every single second of every day to survive—to not stop no matter what. They're not the right soldiers for this war. You are. I need you to stay here awhile longer."

"Is this the right time to ask for a raise?" she asked, grinning past the heavy lump in her stomach.

"If we all survive the coming war, you can have anything you want."

"Deal," she said, scraping the yogurt container clean.

"You should stick with the assassin. The two of you are good together."

Strawberry yogurt squirted out of her mouth. "Sorry." She wiped down the countertop with a napkin. "Uh, what do you mean?"

"Slayer is like you. He knows how to survive, and he doesn't give up."

"I'll pass along that you think he's a stubborn masochist too."

Gaelyn smiled. "He knows. A few months ago, back before you came here, I tried to hire him. He turned me down."

"Really? Why?"

"He gets paid seven figures for single kills. He said I couldn't pay him enough to make it worth his while."

"Well, he's working for you now. What changed?"

Gaelyn tipped his glass to her.

"Me?"

"He likes you."

Alex rolled her eyes. "He's an ass. He tried to convince me to come work for him instead."

"I'm not surprised." Gaelyn chuckled. "The assassin has an eye for talent. And he's smitten with you."

"Assassins don't get smitten. It's against their holy code book or something."

He gave her an indulgent smile. "Of course. Well, then," he said standing. "It looks like the firemen have finished their assessment. Holt is waving me over. Do try to get some sleep, Alexandria, while you still can."

Gaelyn joined Holt and the firemen standing beside the front door. Alex watched them for awhile, while she licked her spoon clean. Lights spun atop the emergency vehicles parked on the driveway, the red and blue beams bouncing off the bald vampire's shiny head. Burnt magic hung heavy in the air—the residue of the spent enchantment thick on her tongue, the vile stench of hatred clogging her lungs. Clearing her throat, she snatched up the phone and dialed home.

"Hey, Alex," her sister's voice answered.

"Sera. Did I wake you?"

"No, I just finished breakfast and was about to head out for a run." Awkward silence. "How are you?"

"Busy."

"Are you still in Zurich?"

"Yep. Look, things are super crazy right now," Alex said.

Assassins, hate groups, magic orbs with apocalyptic tendencies. No, there was no reason to burden Sera with that. She'd want to come to Zurich too, and then who would keep Riley safe? Their little brother was a magic chemist, not a fighter.

"Will you and Riley be all right for awhile without me?" Alex asked.

"Sure. I'll try to remember to feed him when he gets hungry."

Sera sounded upset—or, at the very least, on edge. Alex was too. This was the longest they'd ever been apart, and it felt just wrong.

"After I get back, we'll go hunt down some nasty monster who's wreaking havoc on the city," Alex told her.

"Nasty monsters. Sounds like fun."

"Is Riley there?"

"He's in the shower."

Holt was wiggling his little finger at her. Oh, joy, he wanted to talk.

"Give him a kiss for me," Alex said into the phone. "I'll give you a call again soon. I have to run now. "

"Take care of yourself, Alex."

"You too."

She set the phone back on the stand, then took her time placing the yogurt container neatly into the garbage and washing her spoon. By the time she joined the vampire by the door, he was positively seething.

"You did that on purpose," he growled.

"Me?" She licked a speck of yogurt off her thumb. "I'm just being orderly."

"Orderly? Who do you think you're talking to here? I have to send entire crews to clean up your carnage. And my friends have told me stories of your exploits. In detail."

"It sounds like you're hanging around the wrong sort of friends."

"They're not monsters."

"Of course not. If they were, they'd already be dead."

"You spend one day with the assassin, and you fancy

125

yourself the world's biggest ass kicker."

"I've always kicked ass. I don't need an assassin for that."

"Then what do you need him for?"

"Why, Holt! Are you jealous?" She puckered up her lips and blew him a kiss. "I'm flattered."

The fat vein in his temple bulged. Maybe the sight of her pouty lips had given the vampire an aneurysm. Weirdo.

"But I'm afraid I'm not interested in blood suckers," she finished.

"Oh, really?" He drew in a deep breath, a smile curling up his lips. If he'd had a curly mustache, he would have twirled it around his finger. "Because that's not what I smell."

"And what do you smell?" she asked, against her better judgment.

"Arousal."

Yep, her instincts had been spot on. Bad idea.

"It clings to you like a second skin."

Stupid assassin. She'd have to clock him the next time she saw him.

He only seduced you with his crafty hands in your dreams, the voice in her head pointed out helpfully.

There's more than one way to seduce.

True. And I'll bet he knows them all.

"Hush," she said aloud. Oops.

Holt grinned, showing off some fang. Oh, for pete's sake!

"Prudish, are you? Hmm. I wouldn't have guessed it. Not with the way you dress," he said, licking his lips. "Full body leather." His gaze slid up her legs. "You seem like the type who gets off on men talking dirty to you."

"As with all things, vampire, it's all about the

execution. And yours, I'm afraid, is lacking."

He stiffened.

"Maybe you can ask the assassin to give you some pointers," she suggested.

A low growl rumbled in his chest.

"You might want to get that cough checked out," she told him. "In case you haven't heard, the apocalypse is upon us. You wouldn't want to have to sit out our fight with the techno-zombie horde because you came down with a case of the sniffles."

"You watch too much television."

She shrugged. "There are worse hobbies."

"Like spilling blood?"

"Or drinking it," she shot back.

"Mmm. How about just a nip?" He set his hand over his heart. "I promise I won't tell anyone."

"No, you won't. Because I'm not letting you drink from me."

"Oh, you misunderstand. I wasn't asking." He grinned. "I was offering."

"You want me to drink from you?"

He purred. Gross.

"Wrong again, buster. That's not my scene."

Some humans got off on being bitten by vampires—and biting them back. These were the same people who kept chains in their bedroom and thought horse whips were a fashion accessory.

"I smell vampire," he said, sniffing her neck.

"I've fought a few of them since the last time I showered."

Nowadays, showers were practically an endangered species. She was too busy fighting monsters. And apparently allies. And sexy assassins…

"I heard one of my cousins bit you," Holt said, moving in for another sniff.

Alex punched him in the nose, and he pulled back, roaring.

"You broke my nose!"

She crossed her arms against her chest and tapped her foot. "You're a vampire. It's already healed," she said calmly. "Besides, that's what you get for trying to sniff people."

His hand lowered to his knife.

"Unless you're planning on chopping onions, I highly recommend you don't draw that knife. I don't want to have to explain to Gaelyn why I killed his butler."

"Head of the Household Guard," he ground out.

"Whatever."

Holt's shiny head turned shiny red.

"That's nice," she said. "Are we done here? I anticipate fighting at least a dozen monsters tomorrow and really need my beauty sleep."

"I can see why they call you the Black Plague," he said.

"Yep, that's me."

He's not all that bad looking, the voice in her head said as she turned and walked away. *Maybe you should have taken him up on his offer.*

"He's disgusting. He has blood stains on his collar," Alex muttered.

So do you.

She looked down at her shirt—then realized that she'd just changed it. And that it didn't even have a collar.

Made you look!

Yeah, so she had a twelve year old stuck inside of her. Awesome.

"Vigilante!" Holt called out as she reached the door.

Alex turned around. The vampire was running toward her.

"You've been bitten," he whispered. "You can't go through that without a scratch."

She lifted her hand to the scar on her neck. Except the scar was gone. Her skin felt as smooth as it had ever been.

"I'm immune. Gaelyn cleared me."

He shook his head. "That's just what he told you."

She laughed. "You're messing with me."

"No, I'm not. Gaelyn doesn't want you to have a mental breakdown."

"A breakdown? From what?"

"From finding out the truth."

"This is ridiculous."

He caught her arm as she turned away. "You're being turned."

Alex tried to get a read on her own magic. It was agitated—weird, somehow—but it didn't feel like vampire. Still, she had to ask.

"Turning into a vampire?"

"No. Something else. Something new."

"What?"

He shook his head. "I don't know. But you wouldn't be the first hybrid to pop up in Zurich."

CHAPTER SEVENTEEN
Crimson Nightmare

VAMPIRES PLAGUED ALEX'S dreams. They chased her down the streets of Zurich, blood dripping from their fangs. In the end, when they cornered her outside an old church, she turned and massacred them all. She looked down at the nearest corpse. It was Holt. Grinning, she bent over and feasted on his blood.

Alex woke up screaming. Her heart pounding in her chest, she jumped up and scrambled over to her closet. The taste of blood lingered on her tongue.

"It was just a dream," she told herself as she pulled on her workout clothes. She breathed in deeply, trying to calm her racing pulse. "I'm going to punch that stupid vampire in the face."

But she was as guilty as Holt. She never should have let him mess with her head.

"Hybrid, my ass. Ridiculous." She opened her mouth wide in front of the mirror and slid her finger across her teeth. "Ha! No fangs."

The Dragon Born are immune to vampire venom, said the voice.

"How do you know?"

It projected a noncommittal shrug into her head.

"Who are you?"

We've been over this. I'm you. Or a part of you at least.

"Which part?"

The smart part.

Haha.

Before she could argue with, err, herself further, a knock sounded on the front door. She snatched her running shoes from the floor and went to greet her visitor at—she glanced at the clock—seven in the morning. Who came calling at seven? Maybe it was Holt. She exchanged the shoes in her hands for her sword and reached for the door handle.

Metal sang as another sword lifted to meet her slash. Alex stared through crossed blades into the face of the assassin.

"Do you always answer your door by attacking the person on the other side?" Logan asked.

"I've had a rough night."

"Bad dreams?"

Alex blushed. Damn it. "Uh, yeah," she said quickly. "Vampires were chasing me."

"Well, I'm not a vampire. And I'm not here to attack you. So you can put away the sword."

"You first."

Lifting up his hands with a smile, he stepped back and sheathed his sword. He was dressed for a run, just like she was. Instead of blue and purple, though, his running clothes were black. And he'd strapped bands of knives over them. Alex rolled her eyes. Assassins.

"Something amusing you, Vigilante?"

"You, Slayer. Or, more specifically, your knives."

"Not usually the response my knives elicit, but then most people don't go chasing after assassins either."

"I didn't chase after you. You are on *my* doorstep."

"Only because you haven't invited me in."

"And I'm not going to," she said. "How did you even get past Gaelyn's gate security?"

He arched a smug blond eyebrow at her. Assassin, right. Apparently, her brain hadn't entirely woken up yet. She gave it a nudge. Having a conversations with an assassin was dangerous enough; attempting it while half-awake was just plain stupid.

"You still haven't put away your sword," he said casually, as though he were reminding her to water her plants.

"You still haven't told me what you want," she shot back. "At seven in the morning."

"Alex, you're tense."

"I'm fine."

"Does this have anything to do with your dreams?"

"No."

"Do you want to talk about it?"

"Absolutely not."

He smiled. "You're blushing."

"Am not," she ground out, pushing memories of that other dream out of her mind.

As he reached forward, she moved to block his hand.

"Don't be so nervous, sweetheart," he said and brushed a stray hair from her face.

One of the doors to Gaelyn's house opened, and Holt stepped outside. His eyes scanned the grounds. As soon as he saw Logan's hand on her cheek, he started power-walking over.

"Shit," she muttered.

Logan kept his eyes on her. "Is that vampire coming over to start some trouble?"

"Well…" She glanced at Holt; his eyes had gone red. "I don't think he's coming over to shake your hand."

"Invite me inside."

"Why?"

"Because I'd prefer not to kill a vampire on your doorstep," he said. "If we go inside, he can't follow."

"That invite-only trick only works on demon vampires. Holt's a shapeshifting vampire."

"It's not magic that will keep him out. It's etiquette. If he tries to break into your house, Gaelyn won't be happy."

"He can hear you. Heightened senses," she said under her breath.

"I know. That's why I said it," he replied, loud and clear. "To remind him to behave himself. Now, let me in."

"I had no idea the invite-only trick worked on assassins too."

"The magic doesn't keep me out either," he said. "But I'm an old-fashioned sort of guy. I try not to break into someone's house unless I plan on killing them. That's just good manners."

Alex stole another glance at Holt. He was almost upon them, and he looked angrier than ever. Oh, screw it.

"Get in here," she said, grabbing Logan's hand. She pulled him into the house and swung the door shut after him.

"See? That wasn't so hard."

Setting down her sword, Alex peered out of the peephole. She watched Holt give the front door a long, seething look. As he turned to walk away, she let out the deep breath she hadn't even realized she'd been holding. She spun around and glared at Logan.

"You're insane."

"I'm in good company." He looked around. "Nice place." His lip quivered as his eyes settled on the dresser. "Is that a pink lace bra?"

She kicked the drawer shut. "No."

"You really are a hard ass. You know that, right?"

"I hope you're not here to talk about my ass," she said, crossing her arms against her chest.

"No." His gaze slid down her, smooth as satin.

"Stop it."

"Stop what?"

"You're…ogling."

"Assassins don't ogle," he stated coolly.

"What do you do then?"

He considered that for a moment. "We disarm."

"You really have an answer for everything, don't you?"

"Of course."

"Then tell me why you're here," she said.

"We're working together."

"Not at seven in the morning, we aren't." That was far too early in the day to be playing cloak-and-dagger with an assassin.

"Cloak-and-dagger is not my style."

Had she said that aloud? Damn. She really was tired. A magic energy boost from the Smoothie Elixir would have been mighty excellent right now. Too bad it was half a world away. There were a few smoothie shops here, but they just weren't the same. No one could make a smoothie like a Californian.

"Magical chairs?" she asked him.

"No."

"Ring around the rosie?"

"Are you being purposely facetious?"

134

She shrugged. "Well, you know me."

"You're snarky, reckless, and deadly."

"Precisely." Alex strolled over to the refrigerator and pulled out a bottle of orange juice.

"On my way over, I saw scorch marks on Gaelyn's exterior walls." He stopped to watch her chug the orange juice.

"What?" she asked, wiping her mouth with the back of her hand. She tossed the empty bottle into the trash.

"You drink from the bottle," he said.

"So?"

"It's uncouth."

"Well, don't you have a bucketful of fancy words stored up," she replied. "I didn't grow up in a castle, Prince Charming. And I don't spend my days knitting doilies and primping for the big ball. In case you've forgotten, I kill monsters for a living."

"I haven't forgotten. I do enjoy watching you work."

She took a bite out of a prepackaged waffle. Breakfast was healthy today.

"There's a graceful beauty to the way you kill monsters," he continued. "If you ever decide to go to a ball, save me a dance."

"You're kind of crazy. You know that, right?"

"No crazier than you."

He was giving her that look again—the one that short-circuited her brain. The one that made her reckless. It was time to put this runaway train back on track.

"Scorch marks," she reminded him, heading for the bathroom. She grabbed her toothbrush from the cup. "Yeah, so that was the enchanted ball Daisy put back together for us. It decided it would rather be in pieces after all."

"It exploded?"

She paused in brushing her teeth just long enough to nod.

"I wish I could say that I'm surprised," he said. "But it fits them."

Alex washed out her mouth. "The Convictionites?"

"Yes."

She wiped down her mouth, then turned to him. He was leaning against the doorframe, his running suit dark—like a shadow—beneath the harsh bathroom lights. She wondered if he'd had it specially made to blend with his surroundings. Sport shops probably didn't offer an assassins section.

"I bet you're glad I didn't let you stick that ball in your storage cage," she said. "It might have taken a chunk out of your pretty car when it exploded."

"You like my car?" he asked, bracing his arms across the doorway as she tried to pass him.

"Not really."

When she tried to duck under his arm, he brought it down like a guillotine. She pushed against him, trying to break through—and bounced back instead. Logan's arm scooped around her back, catching her.

"I was being sarcastic. It's a muscle car," she said, her gaze sliding past his bare arms. She willed herself not to see. Looking was almost as bad as touching. And much worse than dreaming.

Hehe, you like his muscles, the voice sang.

Not now, she snapped at it.

Oh, hold me, you sexy assassin! Put your strong, sexy arms around me!

You said 'sexy' twice, she told the voice.

For emphasis.

You're crazy.

Hey, I'm not the one talking to myself.

You claim you're a part of me. So yes, you very much are talking to yourself.

The voice fell silent, and Alex left it to chew that over.

"Are you all right?" Logan asked. "You seemed to zone out for a few seconds there."

"I'm fine." She pointed at the gate he'd made with his arms. "Are you going to let me through, or do I have to pull out my sword?"

"Your sword is beside the door."

"Maybe I have another one hidden in the bathroom."

He gave the tiny room a quick visual scan before looking back at her. "No, you don't. There's a dagger hidden behind that picture on the wall, a band of throwing knives stuck to the underside of the sink, and a hammer tucked inside your medicine cabinet."

How did he even know that? Alex gave him a menacing glare.

"You might want to practice that a bit longer in front of the mirror. Or with me. I could give you pointers..." His voice drifted off.

"If you don't let me pass, I'll give you pointers," she told him.

In a single smooth sweep that resembled a bow more than a retreat, Logan stepped back. "As you wish."

Alex walked into the main room, grabbed her running shoes, and sat down on the edge of her bed to lace them up. "You still haven't told me why you're here."

"During the night, another of the Orbs was stolen," he said.

"Which one?"

"The Otherwordly Orb."

"That leaves just the Sorcery Orb before the Convictionites have the whole set," she said.

"Yes."

Alex double-knotted her laces, then hopped up. "Gaelyn doesn't think they can do anything with the Orbs."

"I wouldn't be so sure. They are crafty." Agitation tainted his tone.

"You've had dealings with them before."

"Yes," he said.

"What are they like?"

"Unpleasant." His knuckles cracked. "Now, are you just going to stand there, or would you like to come with me?"

"I haven't had my morning run yet."

"I thought you might like to take it with me today."

Suddenly, his running clothes made sense. "Did you run here?"

"Yes."

"All the way here?"

He shrugged. "I was in the area."

In the area. Yeah, right. He lived clear across the city, on the other side of the lake.

"How did you know I'd be running about now?" she asked him.

"You run at this time every morning. Like clockwork."

"You've been watching me?"

"Yes."

Gaelyn did warn you that the assassin likes you.

Oh, goody. The voice in her head was back.

I missed you too, mage, it said, blowing her a wet kiss.

"We can run by the lake on our way," Logan said, watching her curiously. Maybe her eyes glossed over when she talked to herself.

"We're going to talk about this," Alex told him. "Now."

"That's precisely what I'm doing," he said. "We'll run until we reach the Convictionites' Zurich hideout. We're going to have a chat with them about the Orbs."

"Not about that. About how you've been watching me," she replied, putting steel into her voice.

He looked at her for a moment, then gave her a crisp nod. "Much better. You almost sounded upset."

She frowned at him.

"Cute," he said.

She sighed. "Why have you been stalking me?"

"Observing from a distance. And it's just what I do when someone new and dangerous comes to town. I scope them out. Learn their habits."

"And their weaknesses?"

"Of course."

"So this is all about work?" she asked.

"Naturally," he said. "Though you are prettier than anyone I've ever had to follow."

"Right." She strapped her sword to her back. "I bet you say that to all the girls."

"I can guarantee that I did not say that to the harpy-vampire hybrid who was the last woman I followed."

Alex swallowed a laugh.

"What is it with vampires?" he asked. "There are more vampire hybrids than any other supernatural hybrid."

"No one knows where all the hybrids are coming from. Or what is turning them." She tried not to think about what Holt had said about her—that she was changing too. "They've just popped up out of nowhere. Gaelyn is trying to figure it out, but he's had no luck so far."

"Are you all right?"

"What?" She realized her hand was over the bite mark on her neck. Even though the scar had almost completely faded, she could feel it. The spot seemed cooler than the surrounding skin, but maybe it was just all in her head. "Sure. I'm fine. Tell me about the Convictionites. They have a hideout here in Zurich?"

"They have a hideout in every major magical city," he told her.

"Even San Francisco?"

"Yes," he said. "Why?"

"That's where I live. My sister and brother are there now."

"The Convictionites talk a lot more than they act," he said. "They don't usually attack supernaturals. They are waiting for the right moment."

"Like getting their hands on all the Orbs of Essence?"

"Exactly," he said darkly.

"Like I said, Gaelyn doesn't think they can do anything with the Orbs."

"Gaelyn is naive. The Convictionites don't do anything without a reason. They wouldn't go to all the trouble of stealing the Orbs if they weren't positive it served their end game."

"And what is their end game?"

"To purge every last supernatural from the face of the earth."

CHAPTER EIGHTEEN

The Convictionites

THEY RAN ALONG the lake, heading toward the city. Gaelyn lived just outside of Zurich—on the eastern shore —an area that had been lovingly dubbed the Gold Coast. The 'gold' referred to both the long hours of sunshine and to the wealth of its residents. It might also have had something to do with the huge number of fairies living there. If there was one supernatural universally loved by the humans, it was the pretty-faced fairies.

Well, almost universally loved.

"What do the Convictionites have against supernaturals?" Alex asked Logan as they ran.

"They consider them to be abominations of nature."

Abominations. The word grated on Alex's nerves like no other. It was the name the Magic Council had assigned all Dragon Born. The Convictionites weren't the only bigots around.

"They preach that magic has tainted this world, disrupting the natural order," he continued. "And that the only way to save humanity is to purge this taint."

"Magic is a part of this world," she said. "You could no

more purge it from the earth than you could evaporate the oceans. Nor would you want to. If magic disappeared, *that* would disrupt the natural order. It would throw the whole world out of sync."

"The extremist mind obliterates rational thought on contact. Logic is the biggest threat to their hatred."

"Yeah," she sighed. "People can be real big idiots."

He glanced at her. "You're speaking from personal experience."

"Yep."

"This has something to do with why you hide your magic, doesn't it?"

Alex kept silent. It seemed like the best idea. Her mouth only ever got her into trouble.

"There aren't a whole lot of supernaturals who can dissolve metal," he said. "Some pixies can, but you don't look like a pixie. Or any other type of fairy for that matter. Some demon-powered vampires can do it, but again, you don't look like them. And you don't seem to have any trouble with sunlight. In fact, the sun doesn't seem to affect you at all. You spend all day chasing after monsters, and you don't have so much as a freckle to show for it."

"Magic sunscreen," she told him.

His jaw hardened. "There's no such thing."

"Sure there is," she lied.

"Your heart rate elevates when you lie."

"I'm running. Of course my heart rate is elevated."

"And you sweat."

"Again, *running*," she emphasized.

"You maintained the same heart rate for ten minutes—until a few seconds ago."

"Maybe I need a break. Are we almost there?" she asked.

"Yes, the hideout is near the opera house," he said. "And you're evading. If you're neither fairy, vampire, or otherwordly, that leaves just one option: you're a mage."

"You're forgetting the more obvious option. The human option."

"But you're not just any mage," he continued, as though she hadn't spoken at all. "You must be something special if you're pretending to be human. Maybe you're part of one of the older mage orders. Their members were very powerful. Most of them have fallen out of favor, though, thanks to their penchant for human and supernatural sacrifices."

"You got me." She threw up her hands. "I'm trying to lure you back to my cult's secret cave so I can sacrifice you to our goddess in exchange for ultimate power. In fact, our cave is overflowing with the bones of our victims. Where do you think all those monsters I take out really end up? I'm sure good old Hugh is down there somewhere—or what's left of him anyway."

"You're doing it again," he told her.

"Doing what?"

"Making jokes."

She shrugged. "It's what I do."

"When you're panicking."

"When I'm breathing," she amended. "This whole thing is ridiculous. I'm human."

"If you say so."

Yeah, he didn't believe her. Since the jokes weren't working, her best course of action was to change the subject.

"So, where are you from?" Alex asked, she hoped casually.

His face was smug. "You want to know more about

me?"

Maybe she should have stuck to the weather. Well, too late now.

"You're not from around here," she said.

"No. I'm from a bit of everywhere. Sydney, New York, Moscow, London, Munich. My family moved around a lot."

"The family that disowned you?" she said stupidly.

"Yes. That's the one."

They'd reached the opera house. Thank goodness. Alex sucked at small talk.

Clouds hung dark and heavy in the sky this morning, but the dreary sky only emphasized the beauty of the building's beige stones and pillars. Statue angels sat perched on the roof, as though they were watching over the city. Logan slowed to a walk as they passed the triple glass doorways.

"Where is the hideout?" she asked, matching his pace.

"Not far."

They ascended the pyramid steps surrounding the opera house, squeezing through openings in the crowd. Wide-eyed spectators had gathered on the steps to watch a group of fairies in multi-colored leotards perform. The fairies jumped, flew, and flittered with balletic grace, their bodies drawing glittery pictures in the air with Fairy Dust. The fairies had everyone mesmerized.

Well, almost everyone.

A small group of people sat at the corner of the steps. They were watching the fairies too, but it was not wonder that shone in their eyes. It was hatred. Not one of those people had a single drop of magic in them, but Alex didn't need to sense their magic to feel the miasma of vile energy coming off of them. They were Convictionites. Alex was so certain of this that she wasn't surprised when Logan angled for them. But she wasn't happy either.

"What are you doing?" she whispered.

"Getting us into the hideout."

"How? By going up to them and asking them to let us walk inside?"

"Basically, yes."

"What happened to sneaking around and bypassing defenses? You're an assassin. That's what you do."

"Usually, yes. But I scoped out their hideout before I came to get you."

"And?"

"And their defenses are too good."

"You kill warlords who have entire armies to protect them," she said.

"I also spend weeks planning those operations. I've known the location of this hideout for two hours. We're in a hurry, aren't we?"

The Convictionites had three of the four Orbs. Of course they were in a hurry.

"And, as a matter of fact, the Convictionites could teach those warlords a thing or two about security," he said. "Their defenses are airtight."

"This is a bad idea," she muttered, more to herself than to him.

Logan slid his arm around her hip. When she shot him an irate look, he said, "Just play along." He synched his strides to hers. "And whatever you do, let me do the talking. We want them to let us into their hideout, not shoot at us."

Alex was thinking of a smart retort, then she realized he was right. Her mouth was constantly getting her into trouble. She'd hate for it to get him into trouble too.

Oh you've got it bad.

Now is really not the time, she told the voice.

Thankfully, it didn't persist. Logan led them over to a man wearing a thin brown belt over white jeans. The sleeves of his button-up shirt—pale blue with a hypnotic pattern of tiny white and brown dots—were rolled up exactly to the elbows. His dark hair was styled down to the last strand. Alex had a feeling that 'obsessive' and 'compulsive' were regular ingredients in his morning coffee.

"That's far enough," Mr. OCD told them.

Logan stopped in front of him. "You're in charge here."

It wasn't a question. Assassins didn't ask questions. Assassins made statements.

"I'm Ben," he said. "I know who you are." He looked at Alex. "Both of you. I just had no idea you were working so…" His eyes darted to the hand Logan had settled on her hip. "…so closely together."

"My interests are aligned with hers," Logan said.

"And what interests are those?"

"A gentleman doesn't kiss and tell."

Ben's eyes widened, his cool facade forgotten. A moment later, it was back. He cleared his throat and said, "Slayer and Black Plague working together. I hope you've arranged for someone to take care of the bodies."

"She's working for Gaelyn," one of his minions piped up. "There's a whole crew to do that."

"So you're one of Gaelyn's lackeys now too?" Ben asked Logan.

"I'm no one's lackey, least of all Gaelyn's. And neither is she." He leaned down, kissing her lightly. He pulled back just far enough to look her in the eyes. "I've made her a better offer." His lips caressed hers as he spoke, tempting and teasing.

Ben chuckled. "I can see that."

Alex ignored him; she ignored all of them. They didn't matter. All that mattered was Logan and that delectable aura. He was so close that it slid and rippled against her magic, electrifying every nerve in her body.

His cheek brushed past hers, and he whispered into her ear, "Alex, whatever you're doing to me, you need to stop." His voice was thick and deep. "Even my self-control has its limits."

"What am I doing?" she whispered back.

"I…I don't know. I've never felt anything like it before." He swallowed hard. "But if you don't stop, I promise you we won't be visiting the Convictionites' hideout."

"What will we be doing?" she asked, her breath stuttering as he kissed her neck.

His eyelashes brushed up and he turned his eyes on her. The burning look in them was answer enough. She should pull away from him now. She shouldn't be sliding her hands down his back—and she most certainly shouldn't be rubbing her magic against him. Shit. Her magic was groping him, and she couldn't make it stop. She didn't even want to make it stop.

Shall I snap you out of it? the voice asked.

Yes, please.

Something cold burst through her chest. The invisible blast of blizzard shot from her to Logan. His fingers dug into her shoulders.

"Are you all right?" she whispered.

"Fine. Thanks for that. Whatever that was." His grip relaxed, and he turned back to face the Convictionites.

"Are you done groping your girlfriend, or would you like a few more minutes?" Ben said, smirking.

A few *more* minutes? Exactly how long had they been

making out in front of everyone?

"Forgive me," Logan said coolly. "I'm sure you understand."

"Oh, yes. I understand, Slayer." Ben's gaze rolled up her body. "I really do."

Yuck. Alex resisted the urge to tell the obsessive-compulsive magic hater that he wasn't her type. And that one of his shirt sleeves was shorter than the other.

"We have a business proposition for you," Logan said quickly, as though he knew her mouth was about to overrule her mind.

"What kind of business proposition?" Ben asked.

"The kind where we give you something you've been looking for."

"You have the last—"

"Let's discuss this somewhere private," Logan cut in, looking pointedly at the nearby gathering of fairies and fairy admirers.

"Right." Ben turned to his crew. "Let's go."

Alex and Logan followed the Convictionites around the side of the opera house, to a rust-colored building. As they followed them through the front door of their hideout, she spotted a black wall plaque with a white silhouette on it. Beneath the silhouette, the words 'White Knight' were written in a rigid, boxy font. Apparently, the security company didn't have any qualms about selling their systems to both factions in a fight.

She didn't sense any magic defenses in the building, which wasn't surprising for a group who hated magic. There were, however, enough technological ones to make her realize that Logan hadn't been exaggerating when he'd said the Convictionites could teach warlords a thing or two when it came to security. It also made her wonder how the hell the two of them were going to get out of there if things went south. Which they always did. Inevitably.

The Convictionites slowly peeled away from the group in pairs, stepping into the offshoot rooms along the central corridor. Many of the rooms held desks with computers on top. One was a kitchen and snack corner. The room across the hall from that contained enough weapons to subdue the district. Maybe there were more somewhere else, being saved for that day they decided to take over the entire city. No, not maybe. There were definitely more. This was a house of hate. When it came to people like these, there were always more weapons. Alex was betting they kept them in the basement. They probably had cages full of guns.

"Your installation is very impressive," Logan commented, his eyes darting from room to room.

His face was neutral, but his aura told her that he was as worried as she was about how they were going to get out of there. First things first, though. Alex had to find the Orbs. She put out her magic feelers, trying to figure out where the Convictionites were keeping them.

"Yes, it is," Ben said smugly. "The best security money can buy. I'd wager even you couldn't break it, Slayer."

Logan gave him a cool smile. "A dangerous wager given my reputation."

Alex's scan came up blank. She couldn't sense the Orbs anywhere in the building. She did feel…interference? Is that what it was? It felt like something was jamming her ability to find magic. She should have at least been able to sense Logan's unusual aura. And her magic. She didn't even feel that. Something weird was going on.

"Yes, your reputation," Ben told Logan. "I was thinking about just that. You've been an assassin for, what, ten years?"

"Something like that."

"And in all that time, you've never once taken a job for us. You have taken jobs against us, however."

Logan shrugged. "Such is business. I don't pick my causes. I pick my paychecks."

"You follow the money?"

"Yes."

Alex felt that weird something. It was somewhere in the building. There was no magic to follow, so her mind followed the silence. The quietest spot in the vicinity—the one most devoid of magic—that was the source of the interference. It had to be. She trailed it through floors and ceilings, up to the peak of the building. It was a device, or maybe an artifact. She couldn't say without seeing it. Slowly, she began to poke at it, looking for a weak spot that she could pull back.

"So you will always take the job with the higher payout?" Ben asked.

"It depends," said Logan.

"On what?"

"I won't take anything I believe has an abnormally high chance of getting me killed."

Ben opened the door at the end of the corridor. It led into the basement. His minions had all gone off to perform other undoubtably sinister tasks, but even so, Alex wasn't going to follow him into the basement. Who knew what was down there. Besides the weapons, of course. She was now certain that there were weapons in the basement—just as she was certain that they should not, under any circumstance, go down there.

Alex pulled furiously at the anti-magic field. The crack of splitting fabric sounded in her mind, and the field ripped open. All the magic in the building snapped and flooded into her. Logan caught her arm before she could slam into the wall.

"Where are you taking us?" he asked the Convictionite.

"To speak to the base leader."

"And his office is in the basement?"

Ben smiled. "He's looking over our latest delivery. Something otherworldy."

Now that the field was down, Alex was acutely aware of every molecule of magic in the building. The Orbs weren't there, but there was something else down there... Vile magic. She didn't know what it was, but she wasn't going anywhere near it.

The Orbs aren't here. It's a trap, Alex tried to project into Logan's head. She'd never been able to project her thoughts before, but she had to try. The Convictionite was too close for her to whisper the warning.

"We'll wait here until he's done," Logan told Ben, proving that his reputation was well-earned.

A savage smile slid across Ben's lips. "You will go where I say, assassin," he said as the hallway filled with armed Convictionites. "Did you honestly expect me to believe that someone who'd spent years going out of his way to take on jobs to thwart our order suddenly decided he wanted to make a deal? Whoever hired you to steal those accursed magic orbs from us will be sorely disappointed. They aren't here."

"We already know that," Alex said.

"Oh, so she can use that tongue for more than playing with Slayer!" Ben sneered at her.

"You won't be using your tongue for anything soon," she said.

Logan caught her hand as it dropped to the knife at her

thigh.

"And what a smart mouth!" Ben chuckled. "I can see why you keep her quiet, Slayer."

Alex tried to knock Logan's hand away, but he held on. She shot him a cold glare.

"A woman like that needs a good beating once in a while to keep her in her place." His eyes gleamed with sick delight. "She probably even enjoys it."

Logan released her hand and looked at her. "Do you want to kill him, or should I?"

Alex drew her sword. "I'll do it. You can have his minions."

"Just promise not to kill him too quickly."

"Oh, I won't." She warmed up her sword arm. "I'm going to give him a good beating first. He'll probably even enjoy it."

Ben took a step back. He didn't seem to like the demented smile she was shining his way.

"We have you outnumbered," he said. "Don't move a muscle, or my people will shoot you."

Alex turned to Logan. "Are you worried?" she asked casually.

"No. If they were going to shoot us, they would have done so already. Obviously, their orders are to take us alive."

"There are many places I can shoot you without killing you. Or your lady companion," Ben said, pointing his gun at her.

"Did he just call me your 'lady companion'?" Alex asked Logan.

"He did."

"Bastard."

She rushed the Convictionite. She knocked the gun

from his hand, then swung her arm back around to punch him in the gut. As her fist hit him, magic burst out of her. A layer of frost spread out from the impact point, washing across his whole body. He let out a weak gasp, then fell flat on his back like a stiff, blue popsicle. Well, that was unexpected.

"The Black Plague!" a Convictionite called out. "She's got magic!"

"Kill the monster!" another shouted.

"Kill the monster!" the rest of them echoed.

Alex looked around for cover, but the only way out of there was down into the basement, where they'd be trapped. And there were probably more of them down there. It's not like they had much of a choice, though. Logan was giving the open door to the basement a wary look. The Convictionites raised their guns in sync.

"Hold your fire!" a voice echoed through the building.

The Convictionites parted, pressing their backs to the walls to make space for the man coming down the corridor. This must have been the base leader Ben had mentioned.

The man moved in crisp strides. He wore a navy-blue business suit, but Alex had a feeling he was ex-military. She'd run into her fair share of them. Mayhem employed a few, men and women who couldn't adjust to normal life. So they silenced their nightmares by killing monsters.

The man walking down the corridor wasn't like them. He was a killer. But he didn't kill to silence his nightmares. He didn't kill for profit. He didn't even kill to make humans safe. He killed because he liked it. Alex could see it in his eyes, and she could feel the cold hatred seeping off of him, a perfume of sweat and death.

The man turned his calculating gaze on Logan. He looked like a patient killer, the sort of person who would give up the quick kill now to strike the bigger blow later.

"It's not too late to redeem yourself," he said, stopping in front of Alex and Logan. "Swear your loyalty to the Convictionites, and all will be forgiven."

"We'd never join your cult," she told him.

"You know nothing," he said, his smile smooth and cruel. "Not even your allies."

Alex looked at Logan, but he was evading her eyes.

"The assassin is not just one of the Convictionites," the man said. "He *is* the Convictionites. Our esteemed leaders' only son. Heir to their legacy."

Then he pressed a gun to her chest and pulled the trigger.

CHAPTER NINETEEN

Iron Cage

WHEN ALEX OPENED her eyes, she wasn't dead. She didn't have a bullet hole through her chest. She wasn't even bleeding. Whatever the base leader had shot her with, it wasn't fatal. But it was nasty. She had a hell of a headache.

She sat on the cold, stone floor. Moisture, thick and stale, hung in the air. The room she was in was hardly larger than a closet. It smelled like squishy green things and—more subtly—of reused rags that had soaked too long in a pail of dirty water.

She pushed herself up. A burst of dizziness exploded inside her head, and she swayed sideways, knocking over an old mop. She caught it before it hit the ground, then set it against the wall. Its handle was cracked, but it was the closest thing to a weapon she had at the moment. Her sword and knives were gone. They'd taken her chain whip too.

The walls were buzzing softly with a deep, magical bass. Her magic. Whatever was in those walls was bouncing her own magic right back at her. It was probably iron, the biggest magic reflector. It was used heavily in mage prisons.

There wasn't enough in this room to incapacitate her, but it had slowed her down. She wouldn't last more than five seconds in a fight, weapons or not.

Alex stumbled toward the cell door, fighting to keep down the acid churning in her stomach. She peered through the bars that covered the slender window cut into the metal door. Outside her cell, splotches of sickly yellow light protruded from the ceiling at regular intervals, doing little to illuminate the dark and dreary hallway.

She uncoiled her magic, slipping it between the iron bars. She slid it down the hall, looking for something—anything—that could help her. She found only cell after cell of iron. The vile magic she'd felt earlier was gone. She scented something familiar and followed the trail, her stomach growing uneasier with every doorway that she passed. Her magic slithered under the door at the end of the hall…then snapped back to her so hard that she hit the wall of her cell.

The taste of his familiar aura still lingered in her mouth, its rich scent like poison on her tongue. She'd been trying really hard not to think about him. If the base leader had spoken the truth…no, he was a liar. He was trying to turn her and Logan against each other.

If only she really believed that.

Metal creaked as one of the doors in the hallway opened. Who was she fooling? It wasn't just any of the doors. It was the door at the end of hall, the only one that didn't bounce magic. Three pairs of footsteps walked down the hall: two heavy, one light. Light like an assassin.

Maybe none of it was true. Maybe he wasn't a Convictionite. Maybe he hadn't betrayed her. They might have been questioning him. And now they were returning him to his cell.

That pitiful hope died when the footsteps stopped in front of her cell, and Logan stepped inside.

"Leave us," he told the two guards, giving them a dismissive wave.

They looked at each other, then left the cell, leaving it open a crack. Alex didn't hear them walk away. They must have been keeping watch outside.

"They don't trust you," she laughed. Or coughed. Laugh-coughed. Her head was spinning too much to think clearly.

Logan crouched down in front of her. "Alex," he whispered, brushing his hand down her cheek. "Your skin is burning."

She gave his hand a sloppy shove. "Don't touch me."

"The iron is affecting you. We have to get you out of here."

She snorted. "Why don't you just tell your new friends to let me go? Or should I say old friends?"

"They are no friends of mine."

"Family then."

"My family disowned me years ago," he said. "I told you that."

"You didn't tell me that they were the ones leading the band of psychopaths trying to exterminate the world's supernatural population."

"I didn't think it was relevant."

She laughed, and acid burned her throat. "You didn't think it was relevant? Really? Because I think it's pretty damn relevant. Especially to someone you're in a relationship with."

"Relationship?" A smile touched his lips. "Are we in a relationship, Alex?"

"A business relationship, you crazy assassin." Talking to

him made her head hurt almost as much as being slapped by her own magic. "And if you're not one of them, why are you walking around free out there while I'm trapped in here?"

"My parents and I had a falling out over my lack of discrimination when it came to choosing clients. They didn't like that I took jobs working for supernaturals since that went against their core principle. Nothing has changed. As far as they're concerned, I'm no longer their son."

"Then why did the Convictionites let you out?" she asked.

"Not the Convictionites. Sarth. That's the base leader."

"Soldier boy?"

"Yes. He thought if he could convince me to swear off my wicked ways and return to my parents' loving embrace —in other words, kill for them—then he'd be looking at a promotion. He made the mistake of announcing who I was to the entire base."

"Mistake because…"

"Because as soon as he took me out of my cell and brought me into the room at the end of the hall to talk, I killed him and his two guards," he said. "Then I told the guards standing outside that Sarth had instructed me to interrogate the prisoner for information on the Orbs."

"The prisoner? You mean me?"

"You're welcome."

"I'm not thanking you," she growled.

"Of course not, sweetheart. You can do that later. After we get out of here."

"I woke up in a cell," she reminded him. "An iron cage."

"Which is wreaking havoc with your magic."

"Yes." She glared at him. "No."

"I saw you turn a man into a human popsicle by punching him, hun. I think it's safe to say the cat's out of the bag."

"There is no cat."

"Of course not. And she can't dissolve metal chains either."

"Are you really going to—"

"Or shatter magic barriers."

"I'm not talking about this."

She tried to stand—but her legs refused to cooperate. Her head felt like it was splitting apart from the inside. Logan took her hands, pulling her to her feet.

"I don't trust you," she said, leaning on him as they walked slowly toward the door. The whole room was spinning in a whirl of yellow and green lights. "You've been keeping important things from me."

"I'm not the only one."

Alex ignored the retort. She didn't want to consider the possibility that he was right.

"I don't trust you," she repeated. "But it seems I have no choice. I need you to escape. I'm in no condition to fight my way out alone. So we'll work together. For now. I'll decide later if I need to kill you."

Logan looked at the trembling finger she'd pushed into his face. The iron was giving her the jitters.

"Are you quite finished now?" he asked her.

Alex stumbled forward and threw up in the corner. She straightened, wiping her mouth with the back of her hand.

"Now I'm finished," she told him.

"Thanks for not throwing up on my shoes."

"You're welcome."

He wrapped his arm around her back, supporting her

as they walked out of the cell. One of the guards opened his mouth to say something, but one hard look from Logan convinced him that keeping quiet was the smarter option.

"They look even more afraid of you than they did before," Alex whispered to him as they walked up the stairs.

"Yes. Their leaders' son is far more frightening than their enemies' assassin."

"So they've just been doing whatever you say?" Alex asked, looking at the exit at the end of the very long corridor. Had it really been so long on the way in?

"Since I walked out of Sarth's office, yes, they've followed what few commands I've given. But it's only a matter of time before they find the bodies."

As if on queue, the base's alarm blared to life, its deafening cry scraping out what was left of Alex's eardrums.

"That would be it," he said as they started moving faster toward the exit. "Have the effects of the iron worn off?"

"Not really," she replied. "Do you have my sword?"

"Yes."

"And my knives?"

"Yes. They look good on me."

Alex nearly laughed, but the pair of Convictionites who jumped in their path sobered her right up. Logan engaged them, while she tried not to fall onto the sword he'd put into her hand. Bullets bounced off the walls of the corridor. The rest of the Convictionite force was closing in. Logan stabbed the two men in front of them, then grabbed Alex's hand and pulled her outside. Night had fallen.

"How long was I unconscious down there?" she asked.

"Most of the day," he said, pushing some garbage dumpsters in front of the door. "This won't hold them long. And there are other exits." His eyes drifted upward.

Logan tugged on her arm, yanking her out of the way

of the storm of Convictionites rappelling down from the upper balcony. She didn't have to wait for him to tell her to start running. Her brain wasn't still muddled enough to stay in that alleyway. And she hadn't recovered enough to be reckless anyway.

"I think I've been shot," Alex said, touching the wet spot on her shoulder.

She ran beside him, following him closely as he darted down another street to avoid a flood of Convictionites.

"You think?"

"My mind's still wonky. It's cut off feeling to most of my body."

"Count yourself lucky," he said. "Because I've definitely been shot, and it hurts like hell."

"They're surrounding us."

"I've noticed."

Their escape options were dying fast. She could feel the Convictionites closing in, their numbers swelling into a swarm. A swarm of nasty, evil hornets. Or zombies. There was nowhere to run, but could they fight?

The Convictionites stepped onto the street, their gunfire lighting them up in a halo of death. There were dozens of them, too many to fight off. Alex's adrenaline kicked into full gear, pumping the magic inside of her into a frenzy. It bubbled and popped beneath her skin, trying to burst out.

But she couldn't let it. Sure, she'd frozen the jerk in the corridor solid, but this was outside. Here, there were witnesses. Witnesses who didn't belong to a hate group. Her face had become famous—or at least infamous—in Zurich. News that the Paranormal Vigilante possessed magic would spread. It would spread to the Magic Council, and they would dig until they figured out what she was.

A bullet whizzed past Logan, barely missing his head. She had only two options: die here, or use her magic to save them—then be killed anyway when the council found out.

Alex couldn't see the Convictionites, but she could hear the song of their hatred growing ever louder. She and Logan were completely surrounded.

CHAPTER TWENTY
Blood and Chocolate

ALEX TOOK A deep breath, channeling the magic inside of her. It rolled and crashed like stormy ocean waves, bubbling beneath her skin. The sweet scent of burning bark tickled her nose. She wound her magic up tighter and tighter. Any second now it would erupt. She needed to push it out in a single, explosive burst that hit all the Convictionites closing in on them.

If only she knew what she was doing. But she'd spent too long hiding her magic in the darkest, deepest corner of herself, where no one would ever find it. She'd never learned to master it. She had no experience and no finesse. All she had was raw power.

That would just have to be enough. She lifted her arms over her head...

"Wait," Logan said, taking her hand. "This way."

He pulled her into the nearest building and closed the door behind them. Outside, boots crunched over stone and low voices rumbled beneath the buzz of a broken streetlamp. Alex waited until the sounds of the Convictionites had faded away, then looked up. They were standing inside a dark foyer. Half a dozen potted plants were tucked into a corner beside the large, open staircase. The soft, feathered fingers of the fern leaves tickled the gold railing.

"Where are we?" she asked Logan.

"Somewhere we can hide until they give up and return to their base," he replied, heading toward the stairs.

Some answer. Wherever they were, it sure looked fancy. Maybe an upscale apartment building. Its ritzy residents wouldn't likely appreciate the intrusion. Maybe one of them had already triggered a silent alarm.

"Is this such a good idea?" she asked as they walked up the stairs. "I mean, what if someone living here sees us and calls the police. Or their private security. That would draw the Convictionites' attention, and then they would storm the building and—"

"Alex."

"Yes?"

"Relax. I live here."

"Your apartment is across the lake. I've been there."

"Yes," he said, staring at her. "You have."

Alex kept climbing the stairs, pushing images of a steamy rooftop rendezvous out of her head. They weren't even real—just a dream that he had no way of knowing about.

"You're blushing," he said.

"Am not. I'm flushed from the whole running-for-our-lives thing."

"I see." He kept his eyes forward, away from her.

"What's wrong?"

"Nothing is wrong."

"You're avoiding looking at me," she said.

"Do you want me to look at you?" he asked, turning to

her. His eyes smoldered with green fire, his stare so intense that she couldn't help but look away.

"Um, so, why do you have two apartments?" she said.

A smile lingered on his lips. "It's just the nature of my work. I often work late, and if I'm on this side of Zurich, I don't feel like trekking across the city to my usual apartment."

"Oh. That makes sense." Unlike her stupid comment.

They'd reached the top floor. At the foot of the dark wooden door sat a beige mat with a picture of three black daggers. Nice.

"Don't get many visitors, do you?" she asked.

He unlocked the door and swung it open. "Wipe your feet. You have blood on your shoes."

"So do you," Alex told the assassin, but she scraped her soles against the prickly mat anyway.

She followed him inside. This apartment wasn't as ostentatious as the District 2 one. It was more subdued. While the other one was ultramodern, this one had a sort of classic charm to it. The furniture was antique and rustic, the walls were covered in wood panels, and the scents of pine needles and wildflowers hung in the air. There was even an old-style oven in the corner of the living room. A pile of wood was stacked up beside it. In short, the apartment looked like a page out of Swiss Chalet Living.

"I like it," she told him. "Though it doesn't look very assassiny."

He pulled the curtains shut. "That's not a word."

"Sure it is," she said, flicking her ponytail over her shoulder. The tip was crusted hard. It might have been dirt, though Alex had a feeling it was blood. Maybe even her own blood.

Logan walked up behind her with whispered steps.

"Can you feel anything?"

Alex reached back to brush her hand across the bullet wound. "It's starting to wake up." She cringed. "And you were right. Not feeling anything is better."

"Come on." He tapped his finger on the dining room table. "Let's take a look at that shoulder."

She sat on the edge of the table, watching as he took out a black box. "That looks ominous."

"First aid kit."

"In assassin colors," she pointed out.

"What can I say? It matched my outfit."

"Which one?" she teased, reaching for the box.

"All of them." He caught her hand and set it on her lap. "Now be still while I look at your wound. It looks like the bullet only grazed the skin."

A sharp jolt of pain shot through her arm.

"Did that hurt?" Logan asked.

The wound thumped in time with her pulse. "No," she said through clenched teeth.

"You're a terrible liar, you know. I can't believe you managed to keep a wrap on your magic for so long. How did you fool everyone?"

"Not everyone is a professional cynic."

"The Magic Council is full of professional cynics," he said.

A sudden jolt shot through her, its icy fingers freezing her heart. "Are you going to tell them?"

"You are a first tier mage."

Alex didn't dispute the statement. She didn't say anything at all.

"The Magic Council requires any mage Tier Five or above to submit to testing," he continued. "The bounty on an unregistered mage is not insignificant."

She slid her hand down to the knife strapped to her thigh. Her heart was pounding so hard in her ears that she could barely hear him speak.

"But it's not worth my time," he finished, dousing her wound in alcohol.

Alex bit down hard on her tongue, swallowing a scream.

"I've run into a few unregistered mages over the years. In our world, magic is power and magic is money. No one hides their magic unless they have a damn good reason." He dabbed gauze softly against her wound. "I won't share your secret."

"But if the Magic Council were to offer you more money…" She stopped. Why was she bringing this up? It would only make him suspicious.

"The Magic Council is nothing but a club of self-righteous dictators. If you ask me, they're almost as bad as the Convictionites. I'm not going to let you be a pawn in their power game." He taped a bandage to her shoulder. "There. All done. Now, if you would be so kind as to do me."

"Uh, sure," she said, sliding off the table.

As he pushed himself up, she checked him out. Checked out his wounds, that was. Not him. Half a dozen tiny tears had decimated the front of his running shirt. They looked too small to be bullet holes, though. More likely, they were shards that had broken off the walls during the Convictionites' storm of bullets.

"Take off your shirt," she told him.

Good call. I think the assassin likes a woman who knows how to take charge.

Alex ignored the voice. Logan lifted his arms and pulled the shirt over his head, tossing it neatly over the back of the nearest chair.

"Yeah, it looks like brick shards," she said quickly, keeping her eyes focused on one wound at a time—and not on his naked chest.

Trees, not forest, she told herself as she slid a sliver of brick out of him.

"So, how long do you think the Convictionites will search the streets before they give up and return to base?" she asked him, dropping the sliver into a metal pan.

"A few hours at least. I did kill their base leader. And you killed his second-in-command."

Alex nodded, trying really hard not to touch anything but the tweezers.

"We should probably spend the night here," he said.

The tweezers slipped from her fingers. Logan peered over the edge of the table.

"You dropped your tool," he said.

"Yeah, sorry about that." She swiped the tweezers off the floor and squirted them once more with alcohol before returning to work. "I…I think I'll be ok if I just hurry to the train station and—"

"Alex."

She looked up—which was a mistake. He was giving her that same smoldering stare again. The one that made her brain disconnect from her body.

"You've been uneasy around me all day," he said. "What happened?"

I dreamed about us getting hot and heavy on your roof terrace.

No, not that. Anything but that.

"You weren't honest with me about who you are," she blurted out.

"Neither were you. I'd say we're even," he replied coolly.

"But you were uneasy before that."

"Assassins make people uneasy."

He laughed. "You're too reckless to be rattled by anyone, even an assassin with my reputation."

Alex shrugged—casually, she hoped.

"You're attracted to me," he said.

"You flatter yourself." She pulled the last shard out of him and dropped it into the pail. "All done," she said with a bright smile.

He caught her by the wrist before she could turn away. "Aren't you forgetting something?"

"What?"

He nodded toward the bottle of alcohol and the pads of gauze.

"Oh, right." She wet a piece of gauze with the alcohol and dabbed the first wound.

"I am too," he said after a few seconds of heavy silence.

She taped a bandage over the wound and moved onto the next one. "Are what?"

"Attracted to you."

"Logan, it's been a long day, and I really don't want to talk about this."

"But it's not just that," he continued. "You're the only person I've known who can survive in my world."

"That might have something to do with your choice of profession."

"We have fun together."

"Nearly getting killed. Repeatedly," she said.

"Come on, Alex. Admit it. We make a great team. And you're having fun too."

"Fine. I'm having fun dodging one near-death experience after the other. I should go get my head examined."

"Your head is just fine. Even your recklessness is rather cute." He winked at her.

She taped the next bandage into place. "Your wounds aren't bleeding as much as I'd expected."

"Residual heightened healing thanks to Daisy's treatment yesterday."

"You've experienced this before?" she asked him.

"Yes, the last time she treated me. It will fade within a day or two."

"That's a neat trick." She wetted another gauze pad.

"We need to talk about this," Logan said as she dabbed the next wound.

"About what?"

"Our relationship."

Her hand slipped, scraping the edge of the wound. He grimaced.

"Sorry," she said and taped on the bandage.

Logan lifted his hand to her cheek, stroking it softy. It felt…nice. Too nice to be real. She dropped her eyes to the last wound, the one close to his shoulder.

"This one is bleeding a bit more than the others," Alex said, more for herself than for him. She had to keep her mind busy. An idle mind wandered to forbidden thoughts.

You're the one forbidding yourself. Which is ridiculous. You need to learn how to have fun, the voice said.

What do you consider fun? she asked.

It mentally nudged her toward Logan. It was a solid nudge too. She bumped against him, her nose brushing against his skin.

"Sorry," she muttered—then froze.

A delicious aroma filled her nose, making her dizzy. Chocolate. Cherries. Something thick and masculine… She slid her cheek down his neck, trying to find the source.

Orange. Leather. Metal… She stopped, dropping her hands from his back.

"What's wrong?" he asked, his breaths shallow and strained.

Alex stared at his wound.

"Bandage it up if it's bothering you." He stroked his hand down her arm.

"It's not that. I…want it." She leaned in, reaching toward the drop of blood dripping down his chest. "I want to lick the blood from your skin."

She tried not to look at it, but it was calling to her, compelling her forward.

"I want to taste it on my tongue," she admitted.

He tensed, which only accentuated every muscle in his body. It wasn't just his blood that was tempting.

"But I won't," she said quickly, drawing away.

"Does this have to do with being bitten by a vampire?" he asked.

"Holt said Gaelyn thinks I'm being turned."

"Turned? I thought your body fought off the vampire venom."

"Not into a vampire. I'm immune."

"Because of your unusual magic?" he asked.

"Who says my magic is unusual?"

"I do. I've come across a lot of supernaturals but never one as extraordinary as you."

"Thanks. I guess?"

He slipped his fingers between hers. "It was a compliment."

"Ok. Yes, because of my magic. Holt says I'm turning."

"Of course he says that. He's trying to get into your pants."

"No, he's right. My magic feels…different. I'm

different. I'm not turning into a vampire, but I'm not entirely myself anymore either. Before that vampire elf bit me, I'd never felt the urge to drink blood. I've been bitten before, but something is different this time."

"The person who bit you was a hybrid. That's different." He pressed his index finger to his chest, catching the drop of blood before it slid between his abs.

"Yes," she agreed.

"Is it just my blood you want?" he asked. "Or have you been sipping from that punk Marek?"

"No, this is the first time I've felt this. And you shouldn't be mean to Marek. He's my friend."

"The dragon summoner gets to spend so much more time with you than I do," he said.

Alex laughed. "You're jealous of Marek? Really?"

"You should be spending time with me instead."

"We're spending time together right now."

"Yes," he said, a roguish gleam shining in his eyes. "Yes, we are." He waved his finger under her nose.

She inhaled deeply, the desire for his blood flooding her with fire. She grabbed his hand. Her mouth opened in anticipation as she pulled it toward her. His blood smelled like hot chocolate. It smelled like spice and amber and leather and orange. It smelled like sex.

She dropped his hand. She couldn't taste his blood. She just couldn't.

Logan slid down from the table. He lifted his hand and wiped his blood across her mouth. It burned slow and steady, supercharging every nerve in her lips, tempting her to taste it. She clenched her fists and fought back.

There was something very primal—beyond reason and resolve—in the blood's call. It saturated her senses, dissolving her defenses from the inside out. Her chest shook and trembled.

Logan stepped behind her, his breath hot against her neck. "Why are you fighting it?" he asked. "Why don't you just have a taste?"

It wasn't just the drop on her lips calling out to her now. It was the blood pulsing through his veins, throbbing with every beat of his heart. A soft moan escaped her mouth.

"You always have to be in such perfect control," Logan said. His fingers traced down her neck.

Goosebumps prickled across her skin, and she dug her nails into her palms. "You don't know what will happen if I taste your blood."

"I have a pretty good idea," he said, massaging slow, deep circles into her back. His lips brushed past hers.

"This is a bad idea," she said.

"No, it's a very good idea."

As he kissed her again, the blood on her lips slid into her mouth. Magic flooded her, plunging and cascading like a thousand churning rapids. Pulling him closer, she kissed him deeply—no longer thinking, just wanting.

His hands caressed her curves in slow, teasing strokes. Then he drew away suddenly. A wicked grin touched his lips, and he tugged her top over her head.

"Cold?" he asked, rubbing her shivering arms.

"No."

She pushed out her hands, slamming him against the window. As she kissed him again, her magic crashed against his aura, and her body exploded with heat.

"Alex?" he said softly as she slumped against him.

She buried her face against his shoulder, too humiliated to meet his eyes.

"Are you—" Something thumped against the window,

and he turned. "What the hell is he doing here?"

Alex lifted her head just enough to look through the window. Marek was standing on the balcony outside. And from the look in his eyes, he'd seen everything.

CHAPTER TWENTY-ONE

The Dragon Summoner

ALEX SLID OPEN the door to the balcony, and Marek stepped inside, fading tendrils of electric-blue magic rolling off of him. The air stank of sulfur and sweat.

"How did you get all the way up here?" she asked, looking down at the street far below.

"I summoned a dragon to fly me up."

That explained the blue magic and the sulfur. It didn't, however, explain what he was doing here in the first place.

"I thought you were in London," she said.

"Gaelyn called me back here on account of the colossal mess you've managed to get yourself into."

He shot a hard look at Logan, who returned the glare twofold and began to tap his fingers across his knives. Alex stepped between them before a fight broke out.

"I'm fine," she assured Marek.

"No, you are *not* fine, Alex," he said, but he wasn't even looking at her. He continued to glare at Logan, his eyes trying to burn a hole through the assassin's forehead. "You are in deep shit, and what's worse is you don't even seem to realize it."

"We're working together," she told him.

"Oh, yes. I can see how hard you're working." His eyes flickered to her. "Nice bra, by the way."

Alex dove for her top, pulling it on over her sports bra.

"Lay off, mage," Logan said, a warning simmering beneath the surface of his words.

Marek didn't fail to notice—or react. "You're oddly protective of Alex for someone who kidnapped her and chained her up in an old factory."

"You are blowing this way out of proportion," Logan replied calmly, folding his arms across his chest.

"Way…out of proportion?" Marek choked on the words like they were poison. "You're mad."

"I'm not the only one. I know what your mother gets up to, mage, and I know all about the sorts of vile things she has you and your brothers do to further your dynasty's interests."

Marek paled. "I don't chain people up."

"I was saving her life. If you're going to come up here and make wild accusations, you could at least bother to get your facts straight first."

"How do you know about that?" Alex asked Marek.

"Gaelyn told me about it. When you started hanging around the assassin, he became concerned for your wellbeing."

"Gaelyn hired him to work with me," she said. And he'd told her that she and Logan made a great team. Marek was just projecting his dislike.

Marek's mouth fell open. When no words escaped, he shut it again.

"Wrong again, mage," Logan said coolly.

Orange flames burst out of Marek's hands, spreading up his arms.

"Really?" Logan expelled a single laugh, harsh and short. "You want to do this here?"

"No, he doesn't," Alex said quickly, then grabbed Marek by the collar of his shiny black leather jacket and pulled him aside. When they were on the other side of the room, she lowered her voice to mutter, "Have you completely lost your mind? You know better than to provoke an assassin on his own turf. He will pulverize you."

"You underestimate me."

Beads of lightning sizzled to life, slithering across the flames. Alex had the sudden urge to blast him with her newfound blizzard trick—but she couldn't. Marek was her friend, and friends didn't deep-freeze friends.

Besides, you're lying to him about your magic. Or lack of magic.

Oh, good. Here I was worrying that you'd gone off and left me, she said to the voice.

It grinned in her mind.

"I'm not underestimating you," she told Marek. "But I've seen him fight. I even fought him myself."

"Did you now? I hope you hurt him."

"I lassoed him with his own chains."

Marek snorted.

"Why do you hate him so much anyway?" she asked.

"I have my reasons."

"Oh, I see," she said, raising her voice. "And these unspecified reasons wouldn't happen to have anything to do with the 'vile things' Logan hinted at, would they?"

Marek pretended to be interested in the stack of wood beside the fireplace.

"Marek?"

He looked at her. "Logan, is it? You're on a first-name basis with the assassin? Really?"

"We only call each other Slayer and Vigilante when we play dress up," Logan said.

Alex swiveled around to stare him down from across the room. "You are not helping."

"I meant in full-battle gear." He shook his head slowly, but delight shone in his eyes. "Wicked girl."

Yeah, she so wasn't going there. She turned back to Marek.

"How did you know where to find us?" she asked, dropping her voice to a whisper again.

"I followed the sounds of gunfire, knowing you'd be at the center of it all."

"Haha."

"Gaelyn is tracking your phone," Marek told her. "When you went into a building this morning and still hadn't come out hours later, he became concerned and called me."

"He didn't become concerned when I was stuck inside the Rote Fabrik all night a couple days ago."

Marek shrugged. "He probably figured you'd found yourself a quirky artist to go home with."

"Yeah, because that sounds just like me."

"Well, considering the way you were kissing the assassin…" His eyes narrowed. "What's got into you?"

"I'm a big girl. I can take care of myself."

"This is precisely what I was talking about before. You're reckless. Of all the assassins in Zurich, why did it have to be Slayer?"

"He's a good kisser."

He frowned at her. "This isn't the time for your jokes, Alex."

She leaned in, dropping her voice further. "Something is happening to me, Marek. Ever since that vampire elf bit me, I've been feeling different."

"Like vampire different?"

"No. Well, not exactly. Besides the thing with the blood."

"Thing with the blood?"

"I was taking care of Logan's wounds. There was some blood. It…called to me. I wanted to taste it. No, not just wanted. I *had* to taste it. It was like a part of me was missing, and drinking his blood would make me whole again."

"Hunger?"

"No," she said, her cheeks burning. "Lust."

"Did you…"

She nodded.

"And what happened?"

"Well, drinking his blood didn't quell the lust. It only kicked it up a few notches."

"That explains a few things." He looked relieved. "You were drunk. It happens to all supernaturals, and each group has its own trigger. For mages, it's spell magic. For fairies, it's that golden nectar they make. For the otherworldly, it's those rivers of ethereal energy that intersect the earth. And for vampires, it's blood."

"I know this already. I've fought my share of magic-drunk supernaturals."

"Knowing it and living it are two entirely different things." He set his hand on her forehead. "Though I have to tell you that you don't feel like a vampire."

Which might have had something to do with her ingrained habit of masking her magic. Still, he was right. She knew what a vampire's magic felt like, and hers wasn't it.

"Holt told me I was turning," she said.

"Holt?" Marek laughed. "Wait a minute. All this panic over blood is because of something Holt told you? That vampire is lusting after you even more than the assassin. I once caught him with a pair of your knickers."

"Gross. Remind me to ask Gaelyn to have my locks changed."

"You let him get into your head, Alex. And then your mind told you that you wanted the blood. It happens all the time to vampire groupies."

"I am not a vampire groupie," she ground out.

"Of course not. But you were bitten by a vampire, and then another vampire whispered into your ear that you were turning. He probably told you that you smelled like vampire."

"Yes."

Marek nodded knowingly. "See? It was all part of Holt's plan to seduce you. The whole thing reeks of vampire arrogance."

"You're suggesting that he told that vampire elf to bite me?"

"No, he's a warped little git, but he's no traitor. However, I could see him taking advantage of a situation like that. He'll be disappointed to learn that another man benefited from the fruits of his labor."

"Holt said Gaelyn knew I was being turned and kept it from me so I wouldn't have a mental breakdown."

"People lie, Alex."

"I know. And I can tell when they do. Holt wasn't lying. He believed what he said."

"Ok." Marek patted her on the back. "Gaelyn hasn't said anything about this to me, but we'll talk to him when this is all over. To be honest, I'm more concerned about your snogging the assassin than your newfound appetite for blood."

"So far it's only been his blood I've wanted."

Marek looked like he'd bitten down on a lemon. "One crisis at a time. Gaelyn tells me that the Convictionites have all four Orbs of Essence. The good news is I know where they've taken them."

"And the bad news?" she asked.

"The bad news is they plan to use them tonight."

CHAPTER TWENTY-TWO
Secrets and Lies

"LOSE THE ASSASSIN," Marek told her. "We have work to do, and he cannot be trusted."

Alex thought about that. Gaelyn had agreed to hire him. They'd been working together for two days, and he'd fought alongside her. He'd even saved her a few times. He hadn't made a single move against her.

Well, except lying to her about who he was. His family was running the organization trying to kill them. Logan said he would help her get the Orbs back, but when push came to shove, would he really take up arms against his own family? He didn't strike her as the sentimental type, but family was family. Marek was right. They couldn't risk trusting him. They were going to invade an enemy stronghold. The odds were against them, and there would be fighting. There was no way to sneak past all the guards. If Logan hesitated to fight back—even for a second—they'd all be dead.

Alex turned around and walked back across the room to Logan. This was going to be a fun conversation.

He was standing right where he'd been before she'd

pulled Marek aside to tell him off—and gotten a stern telling-off herself instead. Logan tracked her progress, a predatory gleam in his eyes.

"Stop watching me like I'm your next target," she told him, trying not to really look at him. Knowing she was going to abandon him made her feel guilty. Though it really shouldn't have. She was doing the right thing. "Yeah, so I'm going with Marek now."

He continued to watch her with that same calculating look in his eyes. Alex squirmed.

"I want to speak with you," he finally said as she was about to turn away.

"Ok. Speak."

"Alone." He gave Marek a pointed look.

"Fine."

He began walking.

"Wait," Marek said, and Logan turned toward him. "Put on a shirt first."

Logan caught the shirt he threw at him. With a cool, liquid smile, he slipped it over his head. Then he waved Alex toward a dark room. As soon as they were inside, he closed the door behind them and flipped the light switch.

Like the living room, this one had a wood floor and wood furniture. Everything was made of oak—old, antique oak. Ancient even. Closets, dressers, a giant canopy bed... Alex nearly choked on her own tongue. He'd brought her to his bedroom.

"Alex."

She looked at him. At the assassin. Most definitely not at the assassin's bed. It seemed...springy. The smile on Logan's lips told her he'd caught her stealing a peek.

"What do you want?" she demanded.

"I overheard your conversation."

"All of it?"

"Yes."

She sighed. Of course he had. Super senses were useful for hunting supernaturals—and eavesdropping on other people's conversations.

"I know that the Convictionites have all four Orbs and plan to use them tonight. You are going after them now. I'm coming with you."

She shook her head. "No."

"Why not?"

"Because I don't trust you."

"The dragon summoner doesn't trust me," he said. "But we've worked together. You know me."

"Do I?" She let out a strained laugh. "Because you lied to me about who you really are. If you lied about that, how can you expect me to trust you about anything else?"

"I'm not the only one who lied about who they are." He stalked forward. "Do you want me to have a guess at what you really are? I have a pretty good idea."

Cold fire burned through her veins. She grew very still, waiting.

"You haven't told him," he said.

Of course she hadn't told Marek. She hadn't told anyone. Marek's mother sat on the Magic Council. Friend or no friend, if he found out what she was, he'd have to report it. The punishment for protecting a Dragon Born mage was severe. Well, she didn't actually know what the punishment was because no one was mad enough to defy the Magic Council. But it was highly unlikely that they showered you in flowers and praises for defying one of their highest mandates.

"It will just be our little secret," Logan told her.

She wondered how much he really knew. Could he

have guessed that she was Dragon Born? The Magic Council kept the details of her kind under wraps, except that they were supposedly extremely dangerous. But Logan had grown up inside an organization that was centuries old. Maybe their records contained accounts of the Dragon Born. Or maybe he was just bluffing when he said he knew what she was. She wasn't willing to risk calling that bluff, though.

"You need me tonight," he said.

"Do we now?"

"Yes. You two are hardly the most subtle individuals. I, on the other hand, know how to sneak into places. Your boy Marek blowing up the front door won't cut it. The Convictionites' numbers are too great for a full-on assault."

"Marek is not my boy."

"Of course not." He reached for her.

Alex stepped aside, evading him. "Stop. We don't have that sort of relationship. And we can't."

"Why not?"

"Again, because I don't trust you."

"Alex," he said seriously. "I've got your back. Believe whatever else you want to about me, but just know that."

She looked into his eyes, pushing her magic past the assassin's mask. He didn't fight her intrusion, though was pretty sure he could have at least tried. She pried and probed and scraped—and probably hurt him a great deal more than she wanted to. Her magic was raw, the result of a great deal of power and zero training in how to use it. He bore it without the slightest reaction whatsoever. Torturing him must have been an exercise in futility.

"I believe you," she finally decided. His aura was speckled with death, but nothing about him reeked of betrayal.

"Then I can come along?"

"You can come along," she agreed.

"Good. That will save me the trouble of tracking you when you leave here."

"Funny."

"Practical," he countered. "Someone has to be there to save you from your own recklessness."

"Like Marek?"

He grabbed a band of throwing knives from his dresser and strapped it across his chest. "No, not Marek. He can't even save himself. He's even more reckless than you."

"I'll tell him you said so."

"Good. Someone needs to," he said, strapping on another band of knives.

"Just how many knives do you think you'll need?" she asked him.

"More than I can carry," he said darkly. "Would you like a few too?"

"No, I'm good. I wouldn't mind a change of clothes, though. Infiltrating a Convictionite base in my running clothes makes me feel…naked."

His brows lifted at the word, but he didn't comment on it. "You could keep a set of your battle leather here. For our future work together."

"Do you anticipate us working together again soon?"

"Yes, I do." His hand brushed down her cheek. "Many times."

She cleared her throat. "Are we still talking about fighting monsters and evil organizations?"

"Of course. What did you think we were talking about?"

"Oh, nothing."

He kissed her lightly on the lips. "We'll talk about *that*

later, when this is all over. Somewhere quiet, maybe a nice dinner. Preferably, without crises popping up all around us."

"That sounds nice, if not impossible."

"We'll just have to make it possible," he said, leaning in for another kiss.

The door quaked with a stampede of pounding fists. Logan drew away from her, his eyes frozen with menace.

"Alex!" Marek shouted through the door. "We're in a hurry! Let's go!"

She pushed down the door handle and stepped out of the bedroom. Logan trailed closely behind, taking her hand as they came into the living room.

Marek's eyes narrowed when he saw their linked hands. "We have a city to save. Say goodbye to your boyfriend because we need to go now."

"He's coming with us," she told him.

"Why? Because he's a good kisser?" Marek demanded, his words laced with ice.

"No, because I can get us inside quietly," Logan said. "Without blowing up the front door and making a big scene."

"There is no front door," said Marek. "The Convictionites have the Orbs on a boat in the middle of Lake Zurich."

CHAPTER TWENTY-THREE
Swimming with Monsters

ALEX STOOD ON the ferry, her hands gripping the cool metal railing, her hair whipping in the wind. She glanced back at the rows of parked cars behind her, then turned to gaze across the lake's dark, glassy surface. She could just make out the silhouette of the Convictionites' ship, a black tear in a beautiful twinkling canvas of night sky.

The ship was floating in the middle of the lake, close to the ferry crossing's halfway point. They were almost there.

A few steps away, in a dark corner beneath the stairs, Logan and Marek were trying to bribe one of the ferry's crew. When Logan handed him a stack of money, the man didn't push it away. He did, however, shake his head in disbelief.

"It's your grave," he said, pocketing the money.

As he turned his back to them, Logan and Marek hurried over to Alex.

"We're good to go," Logan told her, adjusting his wetsuit. "He's going to turn a blind eye when we jump overboard."

"He thinks we're mad." Marek's laugh was strained.

"And he's right. There are monsters in those waters."

"It's our best chance of getting to that ship unnoticed," said Logan. "They would see and hear any boat that tried to approach them. We need the element of surprise."

Marek began to clench and unclench his fist in turn. His face was tight, like he was fighting hard against the urge to shoot swirling balls of destructive magic at the ship.

Logan watched him, apparently unconcerned. "We won't have far to swim."

"Again, I'll say it. There are monsters in those waters. No sane person goes swimming in this part of the lake."

Marek wasn't wrong about that. When magic had come to Zurich, it hadn't spared the lake. Every day, particles of magic seeped off the city's supernatural population, draining into the water, saturating it with the perfume of a hundred thousand magical beings.

Some of the lake's magic was harmless—or even wondrous. Clans of freshwater mermaids lived here. They spent their days sunbathing on the rocks or giving passing boats a playful splash. The water nymphs sang and danced, weaving their seductive spell on anyone foolish enough to stop and watch. The nymphs had their way with the men, then wiped their memories before returning them to land.

And then there were the magical glowing water lilies and swan shifters who lived in the shallow waters near shore. They were moody and loud—the swan shifters, not the water lilies, which were really only pretty. Despite their flair for dramatics, though, the swans were more annoying than threatening. They only preyed on people stupid enough to antagonize them.

So the lakeshore was harmless. The creatures that lived this far out, on the other hand, were in a whole other league.

Alex looked over the edge of the ferry. A school of fish passed by, their scales silver and their eyes glowing an eerie green. The boat cut through a floating debris field. Globs of pulsing, semi-solid goo clung to twigs, leaves, and pieces of discarded garbage.

Monsters stalked the deep waters. Fish with bloody appetites and mouths of daggers. Eels with magic-charged electrical attacks. Sea serpents who had laid claim to larger sections of the lake. They defended their territory without mercy. They didn't even know the meaning of the word.

"Time to go," Logan said.

He and Marek had already climbed over the railing. She joined them.

"I still think I should just summon a water dragon to carry us there," Marek said.

"Save your magic," Alex told him. "You'll most certainly need it before the night is up."

"And you? Won't you need your energy? Swimming is exhausting work."

"I'm used to it," she said.

When the skeptical look on Marek's face persisted, Logan said, "She chased a sea monster from one end of the lake to the other and still had the energy left to kill it. You don't need to worry about her stamina."

"And yours?"

"I'm a triathlete," Logan told him. "And I kill heavily-guarded warlords for a living. You don't need to worry about me either." A cool smile slid across his lips. "But if you're tired, you can crawl onto my back, and I'll carry you there. Alex would be distressed if you were to drown."

Marek sneered at him. "Do you think she'd mind if I blasted you to the bottom of the lake?"

"We're about to sneak aboard an enemy boat," Alex cut

in. "We need to get on, grab the Orbs, and get off—all without getting ourselves killed. There's no room on my team for infighting. You two need to get your shit together and cooperate. Can you handle that?"

"Yes," they said together, still glaring at each other.

"Good. This is your last warning. The next time you two start fighting, I'll tie you together and leave you."

"The Convictionites' ship is packed with armed extremists," Logan said calmly. "Going alone would be reckless."

"When is she not reckless?"

"True."

She glared at them. "Are you done?"

They nodded.

"Ok, let's go."

They let go of the railing and dropped. Cold water crashed against Alex's face as she hit the lake, but she was warm inside her wetsuit. She pushed up, breathing in the night air as she broke the water's surface.

They began swimming toward the boat. A few sea creatures slithered by, but none of them looked hungry. Or at least not hungry enough to fight for their dinner. Thank goodness. Video games made fighting monsters in water look a whole lot easier than it actually was in real life.

Alex tried to keep her strokes smooth and soft, but to her ears their approach sounded like a fight to the death between two opposing sea lion gangs. Drunk sea lions. Wielding high-pressure water cannons.

They reached the ship without getting eaten—or shot. Brushing her fingers across the hull, Alex looked up at the smooth wall looming over them. The deck felt miles away.

"How are we going to get all the way up there?" she whispered.

"Maybe I can make a small hole—" Marek began, tapping his finger against the hull.

"You can think up ways to sink the ship after we get the Orbs back," Logan said.

He pointed at the anchor chain Alex had missed. Man, she was slipping. She really needed to catch a good night's sleep. Or at least a nice, long nap.

Logan was already climbing up the chain, moving like one of those Chinese circus acrobats, like he did this sort of thing every day. He probably did. Breaking and entering enemy strongholds was his specialty. Marek gave the chain a dubious look, then pulled himself up. Alex waited half a minute, then followed.

Particles of rusted metal crusted off the chain as she climbed, sprinkling down into the water like shredded snow. The Convictionites needed to spend less money killing supernaturals and more money on property maintenance.

She reached the top, and slid over the rails, lowering into a crouch beside Logan and Marek. Nearby, two men were chatting, the moonlight lighting up their bright white uniforms. Well, at least the guards on the ship would be easy to spot. What kind of guard wore a white uniform anyway?

Logan tapped a sign on the wall with the White Knight logo on it. Maybe the guards had come with the security package.

Then he pointed at a door that seemed to lead below deck. Right now, they were still in the shadows, but to get to that door, they'd have to pass beneath a well-lit patch of the deck. Someone would have to distract the guards.

As though he'd read her mind, Marek blasted a group of passing eels with a jolt of electrical energy. His spell rolled over them, and they began to circle the ship. Magic sparked and sizzled in the water.

"Hey, have a look at this," one guard told the other, pointing down.

As soon as their backs were turned, Logan ran for the door, his strides as silent as gently falling snow. Alex and Marek followed him, their steps far less stealthy. But it didn't matter at this point. The ship rocked and thumped as the eels bombarded it with electrical magic.

Once Alex and Marek were at the bottom, Logan pulled them under the staircase. A moment later, a dozen guards in pasty-white uniforms stormed up the steps over their heads, rushing toward the deck.

"That is not what we discussed," Logan cut out in a harsh whisper, his cold eyes trained on Marek.

"I diverted their attention."

"You've created a scene. How are we supposed to find the Orbs with the ship on high alert?"

"High alert over a few eels," said Marek.

"Irrelevant. The guards are running around looking for signs of trouble."

"No, they're distracted."

"Stop," Alex cut in. "What's done is done. Let's just find those Orbs and get out of here."

"They're probably on the lowest level," Marek said, peering down the hall. "Villains always keep their stolen plunder on the lowest level. We need to find some stairs leading down."

Logan looked at Alex behind his back. She shook her head and pointed at the floor. The Orbs were on this level. Marek was a first tier mage with some of the most destructive spells she'd ever seen, but he didn't have a nose for magic. He couldn't sniff it out like she could.

"Let's do a pass of this level first," Logan said.

Marek arched a pierced brow at him. "Assassin's intuition?"

"Something like that."

There weren't any more guards in the hallway, so Logan slid quietly from the shadows. Alex followed, stepping into line beside him.

"Which door?" he whispered.

"Sixth one on the right," she said, shivering. "But there's something more behind that door. Vile magic."

"What is it?"

"I don't know. Another magical artifact the Convictionites stole? I felt it at their base this morning, but it was gone when I woke up in the basement. Whatever it is, they must have moved it here."

Marek slid between them. "You look like you know where you're going," he said to Logan, his words dripping with suspicion.

"I heard the guards talking."

Logan's lie was so smooth that even Alex almost believed it. And she knew he was covering for her. She made a mental note never to play poker with him.

They passed through the sixth door, entering a room of shadows. Four orbs, each about the size of a tennis ball, sat on four pedestals at the center of the room, glowing like Christmas lights. Red, blue, gold, and silver—tendrils of magic fire swayed and hummed across the Orbs of Essence.

Behind each of the Orbs stood an iron cage. Gunner, the vampire gang leader from the tournament yesterday, sat motionless inside one of them, his hands covering his head. Blood trickled down his arms, the steady drip of it hitting the floor echoing dully in the hollow chamber.

The champion of the tournament's fairy division, the

golden-haired beauty the admiring crowds had heralded as their 'Fairy Princess', sat in the second cage and wept. Her hair was matted and dirty, her clothes were tattered and torn, and her wings were in shreds.

In the third cage, the ghost of a young girl swirled in stuttered loops, every few seconds throwing herself against the glittery bars. Rather than pass right through, the ghost bounced off and hit the opposite side of the cage. She ricocheted a few more times, then rose up to repeat the sequence again. There was magic in those bars. And that magic, whatever it was, was powerful enough to hold in a non-corporeal being. Alex had only ever once gone ghost hunting. They were hard to catch and damn near impossible to keep trapped.

"White Knight again," Logan said, pointing at the sign attached to the ghost's cage.

"I'm getting sick of seeing that stupid white knight," she replied. "When this is all over and done with, we're going to pay their headquarters a little visit to educate the management on the hazards of selling to radical hate groups."

Marek looked at her. "By hazards, you mean…"

"The hazard of the pointy end of my sword."

"Hold that thought," Logan said. "Someone is coming."

That someone turned out to be a guard. He strode over to the fourth cage—the only one that was empty—and swung the door open. It appeared the Convictionites were ready to return their fourth supernatural victim to his cage, probably after torturing him.

"A mage," she whispered to Logan and Marek. "That's who goes in there. The vampire, the fairy, and the otherworldly are already in their cages."

"Four orbs, four supernaturals. One of each kind," Marek said. "The Convictionites are going to do something to those supernaturals. We need to stop it. Now."

The dull undercurrent of vile magic flared up, and the three caged supernaturals began to scream in agony. Marek screamed too and fell to the ground, his head bouncing off the floor panels with a hollow thump. The stench of acid and decomposing bodies flooded Alex's nose. She pressed her hands over her mouth, willing herself not to throw up.

Marek's limp body began to slide across the floor, as though he were being pulled by an invisible tentacle. Alex grabbed for him, but she was too slow. The invisible tentacle yanked him into the fourth cage and slammed the door shut.

"Marek is the fourth supernatural," she realized.

"Which means we were lured here. I hear five guards in this room and more coming. We need to get out. Now."

"Marek's trapped in that cage. I'm not leaving him. We can't leave the others either. Whatever the Convictionites have planned for them, it's not kisses and cuddles."

"We're outnumbered, Alex," he said with strained patience. "And if we don't go now, we won't be able to at all. We'll be completely pinned in."

"Can't you talk to them?" she asked.

"And what would I say?"

"Command them to stop?"

"That trick won't work a second time," he said. "It only worked before because of the base leader's unchecked ambition."

"Then we fight," she stated.

"All of them?"

She drew her sword. "Yes."

"This is foolish," he said, but drew a pair of knives

anyway.

"I'm going to make a run for those cages and see if I can get them open," she told him.

"The guards will shoot you."

"No, they won't," she said, setting her hand on his. "Because you're going to keep them busy."

"If we survive this, you agree to sit down with me to discuss your recklessness."

"Ok, it's a date. I'll even let you buy me dinner."

"You are a peculiar woman." He kissed her forehead. "But you certainly do know how to motivate a man."

"If I promise to wear the lacy pink lingerie you seemed to like, will that motivate you even more?"

"Yes." He stared at her for a few seconds, his green eyes beautiful and deadly. Shaking his head slowly, he waved her away. "Now let's do this."

Alex waited until he jumped out of the shadows to engage the guards, then she sprinted for the cages. She'd made it halfway there when a mass of lightning, fire, ice, and earth magic exploded on her back. Lights danced across her vision, her feet slipped, and she smacked hard against the ground. Her sword slid across the floor.

Her ears ringing with the aftershocks of the elemental explosion, she peeled her face off the wooden floor to stare down her attacker. But it wasn't a mage the Convictionites had tortured into submission. It was a neat line of a dozen guards, sparkling magic steaming off the barrels of their guns. And every single one of those guns was pointed at her.

Logan lay at their feet, heaving out stuttered breaths. A magical web of silver strands crisscrossed his body, pinning him to the floor.

The guards' line parted, and a woman in a blue business

suit stepped forward, her gold heels clicking and echoing off the walls. She looked down at Logan with cool detachment. When her eyes turned toward Alex, though, rage burned away the ice.

"Who are you, and what are you doing here with my son?" she demanded.

CHAPTER TWENTY-FOUR

Magic Edge

LOGAN'S MOTHER BORE herself with the stately grace of a queen. Her suit was custom-fit, her hands smooth, and her makeup perfect. There wasn't a hair out of place in her blonde bob. As soon as she walked into a room, she owned it. She had a kind of unspoken charisma that just drew people to her, sucking them into the black hole of her soul.

Alex pushed herself up, her back pulsing with pain. She ignored it. She had no intention of confronting the enemy with her face to the floor.

"You should be dead, mage," Logan's mother said, disgust dripping from every word. Her aura smelled like citric acid in a bloody wound.

"Yes, I'm familiar with your little hate group's motto."

She turned her nose up at Alex. Obviously, evil queens didn't appreciate the wit of snarky mercenaries.

"Twelve of my guards shot you," said the Evil Queen. "You got up again. Explain."

Her command was crisp and certain. She was clearly accustomed to people doing whatever she said. Well, Alex was about to disappoint her.

She looked across the line of guards and their guns. Suddenly, the magic artifact she'd found at the tournament made a lot of sense. The Convictionites were a bunch of hypocrites. Go figure.

"You have magic-enchanted weapons," she said. "Explain yourself."

The Evil Queen's pretty little nostrils flared at the order. "How dare you."

"You claim to hate magic."

"Magic is a plague upon this earth," said the Evil Queen, pressing a button on the peculiar device in her hand. "Its taint must be purged."

The vile magic flared up again, stronger than ever. Alex staggered sideways, her head pounding under the pressure. A thick, shimmery film of magic slid over each of the cages. The tentacle that had grabbed Marek had slapped him unconscious; the magic now sizzling across the cages knocked out the other three.

"You're using magic. One of your minions used it at the tournament yesterday. And you're using it now." Alex pointed to the four tendrils of magic—red, blue, gold, and silver—slinking out from the Orbs, licking at the bars of the cages. "Don't you think that's a tad hypocritical?"

"No."

Logan pushed against the magic net pinning him to the ground. It groaned, the strands of silver light blinking faster and faster until they finally snapped. He rose to his feet and turned to stare down his mother.

"Alex is right," he told her.

"You didn't know?" Alex asked.

"No."

The Evil Queen sighed. "Sometimes you need to fight fire with fire, Logan. When all the magic beasts have been purged from the earth, we will destroy the weapons."

"The scary thing is you actually believe that," he said. "But there will always be another battle. Another enemy. I'm remembering now very clearly why I left. Your morality has always been flexible."

"You have no morals, dear. You are an assassin," she said calmly. "An assassin who will take on any client for the right price."

"No, actually. I'd never work for you."

"Logan," Alex said, pointing at the Orbs.

The tendrils linking them to the cages were pulsing faster now. Magic flowed from the four prisoners into the respective Orbs. The Orbs were slurping up their magic.

"What is your game here?" Logan demanded.

"We wait for the Orbs to soak up all the magic they can," said his mother.

"And then?"

"And then we won't ever have to fear those beasts again. All of them—mage, vampire, fairy, and otherworldly—will be at our beck and call."

"The Orbs will allow you to control supernaturals?" he asked.

"Yes."

"How do you know this will work?"

She smiled. "I have my sources."

Maybe her source was lying. Gaelyn wasn't convinced the Orbs held any real power. But considering how quickly they were draining the four supernaturals, Alex wasn't holding out much hope that they were benign.

The other possibility was that the Convictionites' source was telling the truth. But who in the supernatural community knew more about magic than the world's original immortal? And what would possess them to help an organization whose sole purpose was to wipe out magic?

"She's going to use the Orbs to turn the supernaturals against one another," Alex told Logan. "Millions will die—and not just supernaturals. Humans will get caught up in this bloodbath."

"A small price to pay for peace," said the Evil Queen with cool indifference.

"What about your loyal foot soldiers, those poor brainwashed souls who scream out 'death to magic!' as they march in the streets in your hate parades? What would they do if they found out you were using the very magic you'd condemned as evil?"

"They'll never know," she told him. "The simple folk cannot be expected to comprehend the compromises their leaders must make for the greater good. They know only black and white. They cannot understand that magic edge we need to defeat the supernaturals, once and for all."

She was looking at Logan oddly, like he was a bomb waiting to go off. Like he was a weapon. Magic oozed out from the device in her hands, slithering toward him. It smashed against his aura and swirled into it.

"It wasn't just objects that you enhanced with magic," Alex said as the shell of Logan's human aura cracked.

Below, there was magic—lots of magic. It wasn't the naturally occurring sort that she felt from supernaturals. It was like it had been grafted on. It was a thorough job, reaching deep down to the very fabric of his being.

"You've done it with people," she gasped.

Logan's face clenched up, fighting the spread of magic. But he couldn't—not when the magic had come from within.

"What did you do to me?" he growled at his mother.

She pursed her lips and said nothing.

"I wasn't genetically engineered, was I?"

"No, you were enhanced with magic."

"No."

"Yes."

Logan turned to Alex, his brows lifting in question.

"I thought your aura was odd," she said. "But it's not an aura, at least not like humans have them. It's magic. Except it's a mix of human and the supernatural. I've never felt anything like it before. If humans enhanced with magic could exist, I think you're how they would feel."

Logan's jaw tightened, and his hand slid over the knife strapped to his chest.

"We designed you to be the perfect white knight against that black magic," the Evil Queen said. "But then you had to ruin things, betraying your people by running off to kill for profit."

Her eyes were trained on Logan. Alex watched the magic unroll, displacing the broken chips of his cracked human facade. As it slid over his feet, consuming all of him, he stumbled forward onto his knees. Alex ran to him.

"Logan?" she asked, reaching for his shoulder. "Are you all right?"

His hand shot up, catching her by the wrist as his head tilted back. He met her gaze, his eyes glowing a radioactive green.

"Stop," she said, wincing as his grip tightened. The bones in her wrist groaned in protest. "Snap out of it."

"There's no point, dear," the Evil Queen said with a condescending sneer. "That traitor can't hear you. This is our white knight, the one who will purge the world of magic."

Logan lifted Alex up over his hand and tossed her across the room. Her shoulder smashed against the fairy's cage. The magic around it stuttered for a second, then continued to beat on.

"What have you done to him?" she demanded.

"I'm merely setting him straight. I've been too lenient for too long. It's time he set aside his selfish desires and served his family's interests."

"Whether he wants to or not?" Alex said.

The Evil Queen expelled a martyred sigh. "A mother's job is often a thankless one. Some day, he will understand. And then he will thank me."

"You're controlling him, stripping him of his free will," Alex said as a whisper of lime-green dust twinkled between the device and Logan. "With that thing in your hands. If you think he will ever appreciate that, then you don't know your son at all."

"But you do?" the Evil Queen sneered. "No, you know nothing. You are nothing. Just a diversion. He would have grown bored of you soon enough. I've lined up dozens of ladies—all of them beautiful, refined, and respectable. Every one of them eager to be his wife. Not one of them is the least bit like you."

"They sound boring," Alex said, reaching behind her back to slide her hand across the film encasing the fairy's cage. She found a loose edge and began to unravel the spell.

"You are a pest. Your soul is dark," the Evil Queen spat. "Our white knight needs a pure lady."

"You keep saying that. White knight," Alex repeated, noticing the symbol on her device. "White Knight, the security company. They use magic and technology. Just like you."

"Yes, it's one of our subsidiaries," she said with a dismissive wave of her hand.

"You didn't bypass any security to steal the Orbs. You

simply turned it off."

The Evil Queen smirked at her. "We are everywhere. And we will always be a step ahead of you. Always. You cannot win."

Alex gave the film around the fairy's cage a final tug, and it split wide open. The stream of magic that had been draining the fairy whipped back, slamming against the Fairy Orb. The ball fell off the pedestal and hit the floor with a metallic clink, its blue light fizzling out.

"What have you done?!" the Evil Queen roared as the cage clicked open and the fairy fell out.

Alex jumped up and pounded her hands against the ghost's cage. The silver magic snapped and split, and the Otherworldly Orb shot off its pedestal and straight at her. She ducked, and it continued into the open cage, right into the arms of the ghost. The girl dipped her head to Alex in thanks, then disappeared with the Orb.

Hands grabbed Alex from behind, yanking her away from the cages. She kicked against the floor, but his hold was too strong.

"Logan," she said.

He continued to pull her across the room, his arms unyielding, his lips silent. The vile magic his mother had wrapped around him stank of corpses and rust, but beneath it all, she could still smell warm spice, amber, leather, and orange. His scent. She could feel his blood burning hot beneath his skin. She could almost taste it too.

"She's controlling you." Alex pushed her magic against the vile power holding him; it didn't even hiccup. "Wielding you like a weapon."

He didn't react. The Evil Queen was right. He couldn't hear her, not through that shroud of sinister magic. His hold tightened around her chest, pushing the air from her lungs. She kicked his legs and clawed at his arms, but he might as well have been made of iron for all the good it did her. Purple and green lights danced across her eyes.

Wake up! a voice screamed in her ears.

Alex tried to open her eyes, but she saw nothing. She must have blacked out. She tried to move, but she couldn't feel her body.

What's going on? she asked the voice in her head.

Your assassin is suffocating you.

Am I…

Dead? No, I've protected you, the voice told her. *But I can't keep your body alive for long. You need to break the magic holding Logan.*

I tried that already. It's too strong.

It is strong, the voice agreed. *But together we are stronger. I'll help you.*

Who are you?

I'm your dragon.

My…dragon? What does that even mean? she asked it.

I am the dragon part of you. The part that makes you resistant to magic. The part that allows you to sense and break magic. Any magic. We can do this. Trust me. But we need to hurry. Your body won't hold out much longer, and if it dies, we both die.

There are no dragons anymore.

Yes, there are, and you are one of them. So is your sister.

We're Dragon Born.

It's one and the same. You and I are one and the same. The Dragon Born aren't born like dragons. We are the dragons. We have two forms, two sides, two selves: mage and dragon. I am the dragon and you the mage.

Does the Magic Council know?

Once they did. But now I don't know. The voice mentally

slapped her, waking her up as she began to black out again. *We can talk about this later. Right now, I need you to do exactly as I say. I'm going to count to three, and then we'll punch through that magic controlling your assassin.*

Alex didn't argue with the voice. Even if she was crazy —and hearing a voice in your head claiming to be a dragon was as crazy as it got—it wasn't as though she had any better option. She could feel the cold kiss of death hovering over her. Her body was dying.

One, the voice said. *Two. Three!*

Alex pushed out with every drop of magic she had. She could feel the dragon's power intertwining with hers. Magic shot out of her, scorching her nerves and burning her nose. But she could see again at least. As her magic hit Logan, he fell back, but it kept going. It popped like a blown fuse, sucking all the magic out of the room. The last two cages flew open, the Sorcery and Blood Orbs toppled off their pedestals, and Alex swayed sideways. She steadied herself and stalked toward the Evil Queen.

"You cannot win," she spat the Convictionite's words back at her. "Your soul is dark."

Alex glared at the device. Smoke began to rise from its smooth form. The Evil Queen held on for a few seconds before her hands let go of it. She patted them against her skirt.

"You dare attack me," she hissed, raising her hand.

The guards lifted their guns, but when they tried to shoot, nothing happened. The Evil Queen glowered.

"The magic has been sucked out of this room," Alex told her with a casual shrug.

"No." She looked down in disbelief at the Blood Orb at her feet. Its crimson sheen had faded out, leaving only dull metal.

"Kill her!" she shouted as Logan walked up behind Alex.

"I am not your puppet," he ground out.

"You will do as you are told. I made you. Do you know how many of my babies died before we figured out how to get the magic to stick? You are a weapon." Her hateful gaze flickered to Alex. "My weapon against that magic filth. That is your purpose."

"My purpose is what I make it," he said, his eyes promising pain and death. And more pain.

The Evil Queen met his stare for a moment, the contempt seeping off of her almost as potent as his. Then she snatched up the Orb and ducked behind her guards. They tossed down their magic-modified weapons and drew normal guns. They aimed them toward Alex and Logan…

"Get out of my way," Marek growled as he stepped up beside Alex. "I will deal with them." He flipped his palms face up and stared down the guards.

"There's no magic in this room. She said it herself." One of the guards pointed at Alex. "And the magic guns didn't work."

"Oh, look." Purple flames burst out of his hands. "Magic's back."

The guards spun around so hard, some of them collided with one another. They ran for the door.

They didn't make it. A wall of ice shot out of the floor, cutting off their escape. The wave of fire Marek set loose on them did the rest of the job—and it took less than five seconds. Their screams still echoed in the room after their bodies had dissolved into ash.

Alex ran out of the room and up the stairs, but by the time she made it above deck, the Evil Queen and the Blood Orb were nowhere to be seen. Alex didn't feel them either.

They had simply vanished.

CHAPTER TWENTY-FIVE
The Aftermath

BLUE AND RED drawings covered a small section of the deck. The patterns of circles and swirls were faint—and fading fast. The scents of salt and cinnamon hung in the air, tickling Alex's nose.

"Teleportation glyphs," Marek said, walking up beside her. "The ship is empty, by the way."

"The Evil Queen and her minions teleported away?" she asked.

"It appears so."

Logan joined them, his steps heavy and tired. "Evil Queen?"

"Um…"

"It's ok. It's an apt description of her." He looked at Marek. "Can we follow her?"

Marek squatted down and brushed his finger across the glyphs. "It's too late. There's not enough magic left in them."

"Glyphs again?" Alex said, thinking back to the incident with the disappearing unicorns. "Have you asked your mother about them?"

"Yes. She says it's old magic, pretty much forgotten," said Marek. "But a few of the older magic dynasties have the knowledge to create them. My mother is…well, old."

"She can make them?"

He nodded.

"Can you make them work again?"

He shook his head, and his ruffled hair, usually perfectly styled, flopped over his face. He brushed it from his eyes and said, "No. She didn't think I was ready to wield that kind of magic."

"How many mages could weave a spell like this?" she asked.

"In the whole world?" He thought about that for a moment. "Half a dozen mages at most. Maybe a few fairies too."

"Could an enchanted artifact create the glyphs?"

"I don't know."

"Either the Convictionites have an artifact, or a supernatural is helping them."

"No supernatural would help those people." Marek rubbed his head. "They're trying to exterminate our kind."

"Never say never," she said. "Did you get the device she was using to control Logan and the Orbs?"

Marek showed her a warped piece of metal that had melted, then reformed as a shapeless blob. "I'm not sure what we can discern from this broken thing. It looks like it's been through a magic compactor. What happened to it?"

"When the spell over Logan broke, it overloaded." Alex plucked the sorry thing from his hand. "I'll ask Daisy to have a look. She has a knack for fixing magical objects."

"How did the spell overload?" Marek asked, his eyes full of suspicion.

Uh…

"I broke it," Logan told him.

"You?"

"Yes."

"Your mother called you her weapon."

"She'd like to think so," Logan said. "But I choose my own targets."

Marek looked at Alex.

"He helped us," she said.

Marek tapped her bruised wrist, and she winced. "He hurt you."

"The device she used to control him is broken."

"And if she has another?"

"That's why I'm going to ask Daisy to have a look at it. Maybe she can figure out a way to counter it."

Marek sighed. "Alexandria Dering, you are the most reckless person I have ever met. I'm going to get this boat moving. We'll drive it to Gaelyn's house." He walked off toward the glass cabin.

Logan glanced at the fairy and vampire standing nearby, then back at Alex. "Come on," he said, waving for her to follow.

They walked by the glass cabin, where Marek was looking over the various levers and buttons. Alex hoped he knew what he was doing. After the night she'd had, the last thing she needed was to crash into a ferry and have to swim all the way to shore through dark, cold, monster-infested waters.

Logan swiped a box from one of the cabinets they passed and continued on to the other side of the ship. He scanned the area to make sure no one was nearby, then sat down with his back to the wall.

"Let's talk," he said, patting the floor next to him. He

pulled a bag of chips out of the box.

"Is this our talk about my recklessness?" she teased, sitting down across from him.

His brows lifted. "Do you want to discuss your recklessness now?"

"Uh. Not especially."

He opened the bag of chips and offered it to her. "You're not wearing lacy pink lingerie anyway."

"How do you know?" she said with a big smile and grabbed a handful of chips.

"Alex," he said, then stopped. He tapped the knives strapped to his chest, as though he needed them to feel safe. So knives were an assassin's teddybear.

"Logan," she replied, eating one of the chips. It let out a satisfying crack.

He stared at her in silence for a few seconds. The only sounds were the gentle gush of waves sliding against the ship and the cracking of chips.

"I'm sorry," he finally said. "Sorry about what happened. That I hurt you."

He touched her cheek, and she set her hand over his.

"It wasn't your fault," she told him. "You were being controlled. And I could see you fighting the magic."

"I couldn't," he said in a whisper. He stole a glance at Marek, who was still playing with the controls inside the glass cabin. "I lied to him."

"I know. I broke the spell."

"I figured as much. You can break anything. Thank you," he said. "Thank you for doing what I was too weak to do."

"You're strong," she told him. "I always felt something in you. I thought your willpower just gave you a strong aura. But it wasn't that. Your magic is strong. I can feel it now. The magic was always inside of you—beneath the surface, lying in wait. That device unlocked it. Whatever else it did to you, it shattered the barrier hiding your magic."

Logan punched the wall, putting a sizable dent into the metal. His fist came back bloody.

"Logan."

"They lied to me my whole life. Genetically engineered?" He punched the wall again. "I can't believe I fell for that. I was made with magic. What does that even mean? What am I?"

She took his hand before he could punch anything else. "Your magic is unique. You don't feel like anyone I've ever met."

"Will other mages be able to sense me now?" he asked her.

"I'm not sure. Your magic might be different enough that they can't sense it, even the really good Magic Sniffers."

"But you can feel me?"

"Like you, I am different."

And happen to be a dragon, by the way. She didn't share the thought. She wasn't ready. Not yet. She wasn't sure who she was anymore either. Her life had been as much of a life as his. Had Dad known and kept it from her? Or had he been just as ignorant as she?

Logan offered her the bag again. "This wasn't the nice meal I'd had planned, but it will have to do," he said as she ate another handful of chips.

"Do for what?" she asked, licking the salt from her fingers.

He cupped his hands on her cheeks, leaning in to kiss her lightly. She arched forward to follow him as he pulled back.

"There's something between us," he said, looking into her eyes.

She nodded. "I know."

"Are you willing to figure out what it is?" he asked.

"Are you?"

In response, he kissed her again. His hands slid down her back—his touch soothing her bruised body, his lips swallowing her pain. Pulsing with a slow, steady burn, her magic split open, drawing him in. His kiss grew urgent, his magic taut. It slammed against hers, flooding her with heat. She gasped.

Marek cleared his throat loudly. Alex pulled away from Logan and looked up, suddenly cold. She shivered in the late night air.

"We're almost there," he said, giving her a stern look.

"Who's driving the boat?" she asked as she and Logan stood.

"Breena." He said her name like he wanted to write a sonnet about her.

"I didn't know you had a thing for fairies."

"I didn't know you had a thing for assassins," he shot back. "That's twice in one night, Alex."

She planted her hands on her hips. "I can kiss him if I want to."

"That looked like a lot more than kissing," he said, zipping up the back of her wetsuit.

Logan wrapped his arm around her waist. "Do we have a problem?"

"I don't know. Are you going to try to kill her again?"

Logan's hand dropped from her back.

"We've docked," Marek said as the boat rocked. "I need to go and tell Gaelyn's guards to check the ship for any Convictionites who may have hidden below deck."

He didn't have to go looking. The guards were waiting for them as soon as they stepped onto the dock. Most of them boarded the ship, but two stayed behind to help the fairy and the vampire toward the house. Marek followed behind them. Alex and Logan took up the rear.

"Gaelyn wants to speak to you," Marek told Alex, grabbing her hand. He pulled her quickly through the door and toward the ancient immortal, who was standing beside the kitchen bar.

Metal screeched behind her. She spun around just in time to see a cage crash down over Logan, trapping him.

"What's going on?" she demanded as Marek pressed a button that opened up a hole in the floor. It swallowed the cage, lowering it into the basement.

He and Gaelyn exchanged wary glances.

"Explain," she growled at them.

"I called Gaelyn from the ship. We decided this had to be done. The assassin is a threat. He's been engineered and enhanced with magic to kill supernaturals. We can't just let someone like that run around. Enchanting someone with magic is not like enchanting an object. People are living, and there are side effects. You experienced one of those side effects yourself," he said, pointing at her bruised wrist.

"The artifact his mother used to control him has been rendered useless," she said.

"That doesn't mean she hasn't got another," countered Marek. "Logan is a trained assassin enhanced with powerful magic. We don't even understand the full extent of what he can do. We cannot let him go before we figure this out."

Alex turned to Gaelyn. "Do you endorse this?"

"He is dangerous, Alex. Give us some time. We'll figure this out."

"This is ridiculous," she said, storming off.

She passed the fairy and the vampire, who were sitting on the sofa drinking hot healing drinks. Sweet nectar steamed up from the fairy's mug. The smell of blood rose from the vampire's. Alex wasn't even tempted; she was revolted. So she wasn't turning into some weird hybrid after all. She'd only ever wanted Logan's blood.

"We've thwarted the Convictionites' plan for now, but they still got away with the Blood Orb," Marek told Gaelyn. "Could they use it to control the vampires?"

"Yes, if they can fill it with vampire magic. Was it glowing crimson when they escaped with it?"

"No, it wasn't glowing at all. When the device controlling the Orbs broke, the magic streamed back into us. I woke up fully charged."

"Power you used to turn the Convictionite guards to ashes."

"Did you want them to live?" Marek asked.

"I wanted them to talk. We need information."

"Next time I'll try to save one for you."

Alex passed into the hallway, hurrying toward the staircase that led to the basement. Gaelyn's guards were already there, blocking her path. And at the front of them stood Holt.

"Alex," he said, a smug smirk on his face. "Shame about your assassin. If you're looking for a shoulder to cry on—"

"Move," she snarled at him.

"Sorry, but I can't do that, " he said, looking entirely too pleased with the turn of events. "Gaelyn's orders. No one is allowed to see the prisoner."

Alex pivoted around and stalked off. She would find another way.

CHAPTER TWENTY-SIX
Hidden Threat

EARLY IN THE morning a few days later, Alex descended the stairs into the basement. She walked around an assortment of exercise equipment—big, beefy machines with stacks of heavy weights. This was where the house guards bulked up. The sweats of sweat and testosterone hung heavy in the air.

In the far corner of the expansive underground room, past the bodybuilder paradise, a cage was pressed against the wall. Inside, Logan sat on a cot, reading a book. She crossed the room with whispered steps.

They weren't whispered enough.

"How did you get down here?" Logan asked, his eyes lifting from the book.

"The guards decided to take a nap."

He stood from the cot. "Hmm."

"Ok, I decided for them," she admitted. "By putting a sedative into their drinks."

His eyes panned over her running outfit, the hint of a smile touching his lips. "You're missing your morning run."

"I thought we could take it together."

His smile waned. "I wish I could."

"I talked to Gaelyn about letting you go," she said.

"And how did that go for you?"

"Not well," she said, frowning. "Marek got to him first. They don't want me talking to you. And they've posted extra guards at the stairs and all exits."

"I'm flattered."

"They're for me as much as for you. Apparently, Marek has convinced Gaelyn that I might try something reckless."

"That doesn't sound at all like you."

"Marek and Gaelyn think you're a threat." She closed her fingers around the bars. "But they're wrong."

"No, they're right. I was made to hunt and kill supernaturals. That part is still inside of me, lying in wait. If my mother got control over me again... I attacked you." He reached toward her, then quickly retracted his hand.

"Logan."

He shook his head. "No, I won't hurt you. Not ever again. Everyone is better off when I'm stuck in here."

"I'm not better off," she said, squeezing down hard on the bars.

"I'm an assassin, Alex." He set his hands over hers. "I warned you that hanging around me wasn't a good idea."

"You didn't exactly stay away."

"No," he said, laughing under his breath. "I couldn't."

"I couldn't stay away from you either," she told him. "I tried. I told myself that I hated you. I cursed you for always interfering with my jobs, but you weren't really interfering, were you? You were looking out for me."

"You didn't need my help. It was just an excuse to see you. I was always thinking about you," he said, pulling her hand through the bars. "Ever since the day we met, there was just something about you. Something unique. There aren't many people who can mouth off to a pack of werewolves."

"Or to a notorious assassin?"

"Are you goading me?"

"I would never goad the great Slayer." She grinned. "He might show me his knives."

"Your smart mouth is going to get you into trouble," he said, tracing his finger across her lips.

She closed her eyes and slid her magic through the bars. "It already has. It got your attention."

"You have my complete attention right now. What are you doing to me?" he asked, his voice strained.

She pushed her magic against his, grinding it into his soul. "Making sure you remember me when I'm gone."

"Are you going somewhere?" He gave her a rough tug.

"The guards are coming. They won't be happy to find me down here."

He kissed her—long and hard and deliciously sweet—then pulled away from the bars. "Then you should go."

Orange and vanilla teased her tongue. "On second thought, I don't think I'll go. I'm not leaving you here."

"I'll be fine."

"You're in a cage."

"As far as prisons go, Gaelyn's is a luxury resort," he said. "There's even a shower behind the door."

"Logan—"

"You're not safe around me, not until I'm in control of myself again."

"I'm going to figure out what the Convictionites did to you, and I'm going to fix it," Alex promised.

"Don't get yourself into trouble on my account."

"Alex doesn't need your help to find trouble," Marek's voice said.

She turned around to find him standing amongst the exercise machines. His eyes were agitated, his expression resigned.

"She finds it all by herself," he finished with a heavy sigh.

Alex planted her hands on her hips and stared him down. "What do you want?"

The expression on her face must have been pretty murderous because he cringed—which she only felt a little guilty about. Marek was her friend, but he was being a first-rate nincompoop at the moment.

"You drugged the guards." He moved slowly toward her, as though afraid that any sudden movement would set her off.

"You might as well put your hands where I can see them, Marek," she told him. "I can hear the lightning buzzing off your fingertips."

The subtle hum of magic stopped, but the scent of burning dust lingered in the air. Marek swung his hands around and folded them together.

"You're needed upstairs," he said.

"I'm busy," she replied, turning her back on him.

"*Both* of you are needed upstairs."

She spun back around. "You're letting Logan go?"

"Yes," he said as the cell door clicked open.

"Why?" Logan stepped up behind Alex. "I'm a threat."

"You are," Marek agreed. "But we're facing an even greater threat. We need your help."

"My family." Logan's voice scraped like sliding gravel. "They've made their next move."

"Yes," Marek said. "They've tested the Blood Orb on a small group of vampires." He cleared his throat. "In London."

Alex's heart stuttered. "What happened?"

"The vampires ripped apart a twelve-year-old girl. A mage." His magic oozed agony. "Let's go. We need to figure out how to stop them before they strike again."

Then he turned and walked toward the steps.

"Logan?" Alex said as he stalked off after Marek.

"Yes?" he replied in a low growl.

She kept pace beside him. "We're going to stop the Convictionites."

"Yes."

"And if they try to control you, I will break their spell," she promised. "No matter what they throw at us, we will get through it. Together."

She reached toward him. He stared at her hand for a moment, then took it, giving it a squeeze.

"Yes," he said. "Yes, we will."

Author's Note

If you want to be notified when I have a new release, head on over to my website to sign up for my mailing list at http://www.ellasummers.com/newsletter. Your e-mail address will never be shared, and you can unsubscribe at any time.

If you enjoyed *Magic Edge*, I'd really appreciate if you could spread the word. One of the best ways of doing that is by leaving a review wherever you purchased this book. Thank you for your invaluable support!

What's coming next in the series?

Mercenary Magic, the first book in the *Dragon Born Serafina* series, is available now. It follows the adventures of Alex's sister Sera. *Blood Magic*, the second book of *Dragon Born Alexandria*, and *Magic Games*, the second book of *Dragon Born Serafina*, will also be coming soon.

About the Author

Ella Summers has been writing stories for as long as she could read; she's been coming up with tall tales even longer than that. One of her early year masterpieces was a story about a pigtailed princess and her dragon sidekick. Nowadays, she still writes fantasy. She likes books with lots of action, adventure, and romance. When she is not busy writing or spending time with her two young children, she makes the world safe by fighting robots.

Originally from the U.S., Ella currently resides in Switzerland. She is the author of the epic fantasy series *Sorcery and Science* and the urban fantasy series *Dragon Born*.

www.ellasummers.com

47298885R00140

Made in the USA
Lexington, KY
03 December 2015